Taking Back
Beautiful

Devon Hartford

COPYRIGHT NOTICE

Want to find out about my next book before everyone else and get free novellas not available anywhere else? Then sign up for my mailing list!

Sign up here:

http://eepurl.com/B7crf

DEDICATION

To Julie Clarke because flutes are cool too, and for making Stink Foot the guardian that he is.

Taking Back Beautiful

For the first time in her life, Daphne Bowman wants to get in shape. She wants her beauty back and she's determined to get it.

The last thing she's looking for when she signs up for a membership at Body Fitness is a love connection.

Apollo Armstrong is a personal trainer with an emotional hole in his heart that he is trying to fill with the love of a good woman. He's tired of meaningless dates with meaningless women who have nothing to offer but their bodies. He wants a real connection.

From the moment they meet, their connection is electric. But is it enough to keep them together forever?

TAKING BACK BEAUTIFUL is a fast read with loads of sweet and sexy feels, the scorching hot sex you expect, and the happy ending you demand. Both kinds.

Recommended for ages 18+

Chapter 1

APOLLO

"Hey, Dad," I sigh. "How's it hanging? Seen any good lawnmowers lately?"

His tombstone says, James Armstrong 1963-2015.

"You sure picked a nice view." I tip back the bottle in my hand and take a swallow, staring out at the Pacific Ocean from the San Diego hillside where I sit on the green grass.

Next to Dad's name, the brass plaque reads, Michelle Armstrong 1963-

Hopefully she has plenty of years left in her. Hopefully. But once one of your parents kicks the bucket, you realize the clock is ticking for the other. And for you.

"Hey, you remember Coach Ferguson? From high school football? I ran into him the other day at the grocery store. You know what he told me? His dad was going in for knee surgery. The Ferg was worried that his old man might need to use a walker the rest of his life because he's 82." I smirk and laugh. "82. Can you believe that?"

James Armstrong 1963-2015

52 years old.

2 months gone.

Died Christmas Eve.

I laugh morbidly, "You know you ruined Christmas?" I take another swallow from my bottle. "Mom was crushed. We didn't even open presents. Too bad for you. Did you know Mom finally broke down and bought you season tickets to see the Chargers? The ones you said were too expensive? Would you believe she scored two seats on the railing at club level for next season? 45 yard line. Three grand each. One for you and one for her. Can you believe it? Yeah, I couldn't believe it either. Because I know something you don't. Mom *hates* football. She bought those tickets for you, Dad." I take another drink. I smile sourly. "Guess I'll have to take her. Your loss." I laugh.

It's not a happy laugh.

I take another swallow.

"Want some of this, Dad?" I pour a splash on the grass below his tombstone.

"I don't know how you lucked out finding Mom. In high school no less." I shake my head. "The women I date are so shallow. They care more about expensive purses than they do people. I don't know how I pick 'em. I must be a bad judge of character. The last girl I was seeing was sleeping with three other guys. I wasn't getting sloppy seconds. I was getting sloppy fourths. Can you believe that? If you were still around, I'd start bringing my dates over to you and Mom's house so you guys could give me a thumbs up or down."

My eyes water.

"But you're gone." The words come out in a hoarse hiss. "I miss you, Dad."

"Is your daddy in heaven too?"

I look up into the eyes of some kid I've never seen before. He wears an Angry Birds shirt and looks like he's five. "Yeah," I mutter.

"So's mine."

"Sorry to hear that. Do you miss him?"

"Uh huh."

"Me too," I sigh.

"Don't be sad. Mommy says he's with you right now. He's with you every day. In your heart." He touches his chest with one little pink finger.

"Yeah." I choke out the word and hang my head. My eyes are all wet.

"I'm firsty. Can I have some of your water?"

"Sorry, kid. It's… medicine." I wrap my fingers over the SMIRNOFF logo.

"I don't like medicine."

"Me neither."

"But Mommy says I have to take it even if I don't like it. She says it'll make me feel better."

I smirk, "Your mommy is right."

The kid nods, "Then you better drink your medicine."

"Yeah." I swig a swallow of vodka.

"There you are, Owen," the most beautiful woman I've ever seen says to the kid. She looks at me with concern, then back at her son. "What are you doing over here, Owen?"

I set my bottle in the grass to my right, so she can't see it.

Owen says, "He lost his daddy too."

She smiles at me, eyes full of compassion. The most beautiful eyes I've ever seen. "I'm so sorry. Was it recently?"

I nod. "Two months ago."

Her eyes soften, "I'm so sorry. It must be very hard for you."

I want to pour my heart out to this beautiful angel. "Yeah."

"My daddy died when I was only a baby," Owen says. The mom kneels beside him and rubs his back. "Don't be sad," Owen says. "Maybe you'll get a new daddy like I did."

I frown, confused.

The mom says, "He means—"

"Hey guys," a dude with wireframe glasses says to the Mom and the kid.

"See?" Owen says. "I have two daddies who love me."

The dude kneels down beside the boy and hugs him to his side. "That's right, Owen. I love you very much." He glances at me.

I look like a mess. I know it.

The dude says, "We should probably get going."

I don't blame him for wanting to get as far away from me as possible. Because I'm looking at his wife like I wish she was mine.

The dude and his wife stand up. The wife says, "Do you have anyone you can talk to?"

I almost laugh. Do I look that pathetic right now? "Yeah, my Mom. She's still healthy as a horse."

The wife nods, "That's good. You should call her. Or something."

"Yeah. I'm seeing her this weekend."

She nods and smiles, "Oh, good. Owen, say goodbye to the nice man."

Owen waves his little hand, "Bye! And don't forget to drink your medicine!"

The mom laughs, "What?"

"He has medicine, Mommy. I asked him for some because I was firsty."

Great. Now I look like a total loser.

"It's water," I say, cradling the bottle of vodka against my hip, praying to God they won't see it and ask any more questions.

"Take it easy," the dude, Dad #2, says.

I salute them. "Yeah. You guys too. Drive safe. To wherever you're going."

"Will do," the dad says as they walk off, "and take care of yourself."

"Yeah," I laugh.

At least they know where they're going.

Because I sure don't.

Chapter 2

DAPHNE

Today is the day I take my beauty back.

For me.

I open the door of Body Fitness and walk inside.

The lobby is flashy and colorful and fun. I've heard that movie stars and models go here. It's all so exciting.

I'm wearing the cute new workout outfit I bought at Lane Bryant just for the occasion. I swear it feels ten times tighter than it did when I tried it on in the store. But I think that's just my nerves because both the loose fitting active Tee and print leggings have plenty of give.

This is the first time I've set foot in a gym since I graduated from North Valley High School. Back then, I only went to the gym because I was forced to for PE class. I hated PE. Me and exercise have never been friends. You know those girls in grade school who always got picked last for team sports? I was that girl.

Now I'm the adult version of her.

But you know what?

I'm going to change that.

Today.

They always say it's never too late to start exercising and I'm only 29. Why not now? I can meet 30 head on with a better body.

As I stand in the lobby, people come and go through the front doors. It's 6 o'clock, so I imagine everyone here is doing their post-work workouts like I am. I'm an administrative assistant slash receptionist for a dentist in Van Nuys. It pays the bills. Anyway, I had to leave the office a half hour early to make it here on time.

I can't help noticing that everyone passing me is so much thinner than I am. What am I even doing here? Gyms like this are for beautiful people. Maybe I should've signed up for a membership at Curves instead.

No.

I'm not giving up on myself that easily.

And I'm not hiding myself. Because I'm not ugly. I just have a few too many extra pounds that I can't seem to get rid of. There's a beautiful body underneath my comfy cushions and errant stretch marks.

This is my first actual workout since I signed up for a trial membership last week. I also have an appointment with a personal trainer this evening because I don't know the first thing about exercise or working out. I don't know who my trainer is, but the sales guy who signed me up told me their staff of trainers is the best in Los Angeles. Hopefully my trainer will be a nice woman. Someone motherly. I need all the moral support I can get if I'm going to do this. If it's a man, I don't know what I'll do. Ever since I can remember, boys have always made me nervous. They still do.

My heart pounds as I walk up to the oblong reception counter to sign in.

The rail-thin receptionist behind the counter is stunning. She has a fashion model body and weighs maybe forty pounds. It's her genetics. She has bird bones and I have... bear bones. She wears a purple Body Fitness polo shirt that is tight across her perfectly perky breasts which are probably fake. In her case, it should be perky *beasts* because it reflects her monstrous personality. Anyway, I wish I could wear a shirt that tight. Perky breasts have never been my style. Not by choice.

I wait for her to notice me.

She doesn't seem to.

I wait patiently.

She still doesn't notice.

"Excuse me?" I mutter.

She doesn't hear me.

"Um, excuse me?"

Without making eye contact, she says, "One second." She spins and walks into the glass office behind the counter.

People tend to ignore me like this. I'm used to it. I wait patiently. While I wait, more beautiful people swipe their cards under a laser scanner and walk straight into the gym.

They belong here.

I don't.

NO!

Why do I always do this to myself? I belong here as much as anyone else!

The perky-breasted receptionist is chatting with a handsome guy in the glass office. The kind of guy who never ever talks to me unless I'm buying something from him. Both of them laugh. The receptionist glances at me momentarily. She really is beautiful enough to be a model. Again, genetics. The two of them continue to chatter away.

Geesh. I'm not supposed to enter the gym proper until I sign in. I still don't have a permanent card because I'm a trial member. At this rate, I'm going to cancel my membership before the trial period is even over. I'm also going to be late for my appointment with my trainer. But Fashion Forty and Office Guy don't notice because they're busy jabbering away. I can't overhear what they're saying, but I can imagine it.

Him: "Can you believe she came back?"

Her: "No way."

Him: "I thought she was gonna be one of those pipe-dream New Year's Resolution people who never come back after they sign up."

Her: "She *shouldn't* have come back. What an embarrassment. Is it too late to decline her membership application? She might scare off the other members."

Him: "Are you kidding? She'll be comedy relief for everyone. Sign her in. After you do, we can watch her make a fool of herself on the security cameras in my office. It'll be a laugh."

Fashion Forty giggles at him, then perches her tiny behind on the edge of Handsome Office Guy's desk, a.k.a. HOG, with her back completely to me. Did I mention that HOG looks like every jerky guy on the high school football team when I was at North Valley? The ones who always made fun of me? Of course he does.

My face burns with embarrassment. I'm ready to turn around and leave.

No!

I remind myself I didn't actually hear what they were saying. I was making all of that up in my own head. If there's one thing I've learned in life, it's that I'm usually my own worst enemy.

I'm not leaving.

I will wait however long it takes.

Fashion Forty continues chatting with HOG. Is she ever going to sign me in?

"Excuse me," I call out in a strong voice.

Fashion Forty and HOG ignore me.

"Excuse me!" I yell, my face now hot with anger.

Fashion Forty is still ignoring me.

"Ex-CUSE—!"

"Is anybody helping you?" a gruff voice says behind me.

Startled, I turn around and stare right at a solid wall of purple. I tilt my head up and realize it's a purple Body Fitness polo shirt wrapped around a man mountain. As my gaze climbs higher, I realize it's a man Mount Olympus because there's a god on top. Chiseled features, just enough scruff, short thick unruly dark hair, honey gold eyes that glow like sunshine and a panty melting smile as hot as the surface of the sun.

And yes, that smile is aimed at me.

My heart races. I can't speak.

His smile curls, "Is… is anybody helping you?"

I swallow hard and my throat clicks. "Ummm…"

"Is this your first time here?" His eyes glimmer and my brain melts.

That voice.

It's music.

Have you ever been to the symphony? I went once. On a field trip in middle school because I was in orchestra class. At the time, I played flute because my mom told me it was a girl's instrument. So I played flute. But then my orchestra class took that field trip. We were bussed downtown to the Los Angeles Philharmonic to watch the world-famous cellist Yo Yo Ma play Bach's six cello suites. When Yo Yo Ma drew his bow across the strings and played the prelude of Cello Suite No. 1, I was mesmerized from the first note. It's the piece you always hear at weddings before the bride arrives. It's both celebratory and melancholy at the same time. I can't think of a more beautiful piece of music in the world. That sound did something to my little twelve year old self that I couldn't explain. I latched onto that melancholy and joy like it was my own. It was the most uplifting and beautiful thing I'd ever heard. When I got home that night, the first thing I did was tell my mom I was changing my instrument from flute to cello. We had a huge fight. But I wouldn't back down. It was probably the first time I ever stood up to her over something important. Anything, for that matter. She finally relented and I've been playing cello ever since. To this day, the sound of cellos playing is my favorite thing.

"I said, is this your first time here?" the godlike man asks again.

That voice isn't mere music.

That voice is those cellos.

It rocks me to my core.

"Ummmm…" I titter.

Any second, I'm going to start crying or laughing. This man's voice is my soulmate. Ridiculous but true. This revelation hurts like you can't imagine because a man this handsome will never give a damn about me. That's just the way it is. I'm surprised he's even talking to me.

Behind me, I hear Fashion Forty laugh in the glass office with HOG. The sound of their voices is like breaking glass and it's ugly and awful. Their sound is the one I'm accustomed to. Not cellos.

I start to shake with disappointment and sadness.

I want to run away from this place and never come back. I grab one last look at Mr. Cello's sunshine eyes before I dash out of here so I can remember this moment. At least I'll have that much. Because what's going to happen next is, he's going to walk behind the counter and join Fashion Forty and the HOG in his glass office, and all three of them will point at me and laugh like broken glass.

"Don't worry," Mr. Cello says, his voice rivaling Yo Yo Ma's virtuosity for its beauty. "I can check you in." He walks behind the counter to a computer. "What's your name?"

"Daphne Bowman?" I sound so insecure, like I'm not even sure of my own name. But I always sound this way around men. Especially godlike cello-voiced men like this man.

He clicks keys and the computer beeps. It's the most beautiful beep I've ever heard. "Okay, you're all set. Have a good workout," he smiles.

"Um?" That's all I can force out.

"Yeah?"

"Um?"

He snickers, "Yes?"

"Um, um, um!" *Get a hold of yourself, Daphne! Use your words!* "Um, I'm supposed to meet with my trainer! At six!" I'm practically shouting.

He's startled.

"Sorry," I sigh.

"It's okay. This is your first time, isn't it?"

"How can you tell?" I ask sarcastically.

He flashes a rugged grin, "You seem a little nervous." The way he's looking at me does something I don't understand. Guys never look at me this way. It's like he *wants* to talk to me.

"Yeah, a little."

Unlike me, he is totally at ease and confident. His shoulders beneath his purple polo are broad and his bare arms defined. "Let's see who your trainer is." He clicks more keys on the computer. He frowns. "I don't see your name on here. Did you reply to the confirmation email we sent out? If you don't, the system automatically fills your slot with someone else."

"No." Crap. That's how these things always work out for me. I forget one little thing and set myself up for daily failure. Now he's going to tell me to go home and never come back.

He smiles, "That's okay. I don't have an appointment until seven. You can be mine."

Did he just say I can be his? I shake my head. *He didn't mean it that way, Daphne. He just means the appointment way. He's just being polite.*

But the flushed look on his face says the opposite. He says, "I mean, you can be my six o'clock. Appointment. My six o'clock appointment." He chuckles.

Nervously.

It sounds like cellos.

APOLLO

"I just need a minute to drop my bag in the locker room," I say to Daphne.

"Okay. Should I wait here?"

"Sure. I'll be right back."

"I'll be here," she smiles.

"Yeah…" I don't know what it is, but that smile is killing me. And those curves. I just want to grab them and never let go. And that smokey black hair of hers tied back in a pony tail that is begging me to wrap my fist around it while I take her from behind. And those liquid blue diamond eyes. It's like they're piercing a hole in my heart. It almost hurts. It's also turning me on, which is weird because I'm not usually an eye man. But I am now. I could stare into her eyes day and night and never get tired of them.

"Weren't you going to the locker room to drop off your bag?"

"Oh, right." *I am such a tool.* "Hold on." I turn and walk fast toward the locker room.

Why am I rushing?

It's not like she's going to leave.

Is she?

When I turn the corner, I speed up and beeline into the men's locker room. I open an empty locker and toss my bag inside. I pull out my padlock from the zipper pocket and hang it on the latch. Then I unzip the big pouch and unscrew the SMIRNOFF without pulling it out of the bag.

For a second I consider not drinking any.

I already had enough at the cemetery. I can't believe I didn't get pulled over by Highway Patrol on the drive up from San Diego. Fuck it. I'm nervous all of a sudden because of Daphne and there's no cops waiting to write me up for DUI here at the gym.

I pull my entire gym bag out of the locker, unscrew the cap on the vodka, and tip it and my gym bag back while I take a swallow. I must look like a high-class wino, drinking from a bottle in an expensive gym bag instead of a greasy paper sack. Whatever. I screw the cap back on and pull out my mint breath freshener and spritz some into my mouth. I breathe on my hand. Mint. I hope she doesn't notice the vodka.

I slam the locker shut and close the padlock.

This day started out in the shitter, but somehow it got turned around.

Somehow being Daphne Bowman.

Chapter 3

DAPHNE

"Are you ready to get pumped?" Apollo asks as he comes strolling back to the reception desk.

WHAT?!?!

My eyes nearly jump out of my face. "Uhhhh…"

What kind of pumped does he mean?

The look in his eye inclines me to believe he means the only kind of pumping a woman wants from a man like him.

Oh. My. Gasp!

Yes, *that* kind of pumping.

The kind that requires the sort of fire hose a man like this obviously keeps coiled in his black khaki shorts.

Okay, he must be blind. That's it. Mr. Cello is blind. It's the only explanation for why he's treating me this way. That's fine with me. I don't judge. Blind is fine.

He smiles, "I like your top, by the way. That shade of blue looks good on you. It brings out your eyes."

Okay, he's not blind.

Died. Gone to Heaven.

"Long time no see," a familiar and irritatingly glassy voice purrs behind me. Fashion Forty. She must've walked out of the office when I wasn't looking. She walks right up to Mr. Cello. Sure, she walks out for him. But me? Of course not.

"Hey, Fiona," Mr. Cello grins at her.

Died. Gone to Hell.

Fashion Forty brushes her fingers across Mr. Cello's muscled forearm. "What's new with you?"

He smiles, about to speak…

This is the moment where my fantasy bubble bursts. Mr. Cello is going to sweep Fashion Forty Fiona off her feet like a feather because she weighs ounces, carry her into the back, and make sweet beautiful people love to her while I stand here like an imbecile. Then HOG will come out of his office long enough to rip up my membership contract, send me on my way, and tell me never to come back. Which, at this point, I will gladly do.

Mr. Cello places his palm against my lower back and says, "I was just about to take Daphne here onto the floor and coach her through her first workout."

I almost have a stroke because his hand is touching me. Despite the insulation of my loose-fitting workout top between his hand and my skin, his touch is making every cell in my body sizzle. The electric sensation emanates out from his hand in pulsating waves. If he doesn't remove it, I'm going to faint.

Fashion Forty scowls at me and deflates. "Oh."

Take that, you heathen! I'm surprised I still haven't fainted because this is now officially the longest amount of time a gorgeous man has touched me. And in a slightly possessive sort of way, no less.

"Let's go, Daphne." Cellos.

"Talk later?" Fashion Forty asks him hopefully.

"I'll see if I have time." Mr. Cello says it like he's saying, *I really won't have time so don't hold your breath.*

I faint.

But somehow I manage to stay on my legs as Mr. Cello guides me toward the workout floor. The sound of whirring ellipticals and stationary bicycles and treadmills is loud. There's a flurry of people moving on the machines, sweating, listening to music on earbuds, reading things on their smart phones, watching the TVs hung from the ceiling. Beyond them, a huge wall of windows reveals the setting sun.

"Sorry about her," Mr. Cello whispers. His hand is still on my back.

"Who? What?" I can't remember what happened a second ago because his touch has blocked out everything else.

"Fiona? The receptionist?"

"Oh, her! I forgot about her!" I giggle.

He smirks, "She's very forgettable."

Huh? Let's be honest. Fashion Forty Fiona is gorgeous. I'm not blind either. When I arrived earlier, the guys checking in were all staring at her. I need to call him on his dishonesty. "What do you mean?"

He rolls his eyes. "Fiona is rude to everybody she doesn't like, which is most people. If it was me, I'd fire her."

"Oh. Really?"

"I saw the way she ignored you when she was in the office with Tony."

"You did?"

He nods, "She does that kind of thing all the time. It's totally unprofessional."

I almost blurt, *So it wasn't just me she was ignoring?* But I manage to keep that to myself. "Right."

"We should have you warm up for a few minutes with some cardio before we start. Get your blood flowing."

Is he kidding? Just being in his presence has my blood flowing just fine. "Okay."

"What do you prefer?"

All I can think is: which machine will make me jiggle the least? Now I'm embarrassed. Why did I have to buy lycra leggings? Couldn't I have bought a tent?

No!

I look good.

I don't need a tent.

"Ummm, whichever?"

He scans the cardio machines. "Let's do the treadmill. There's two free over there. I'll walk next to you."

Is it normal for the trainer to exercise with you? I have no idea. If I'm being logical, I want to say no. I mean, they probably train people all day long all week long. It doesn't make sense that they would be exercising with their clients the whole time. They'd be all sweaty and gross before the day was over. So what in the Eff is he doing offering to walk with me?

I'm not gonna ask.

"Okay!" I blurt.

He leads me to the two treadmills and we both start walking.

I do my best not to bounce. Just thinking about it makes me twice as nervous as I already am. I need a distraction.

As a dental receptionist, I'm used to making small talk. Putting other people at ease is part of my job. I just have a hard time putting myself at ease. So I start talking about anything and everything to Mr. Cello. Before I know it, we're talking like best friends. I can tell you that this isn't normal. Putting people at ease with small talk is one thing. Having a genuinely enjoyable conversation is entirely another. But it's happening between me and Mr. Cello. When I realize this, I go back to being nervous again. I blurt the next thing that comes to mind, otherwise I'm going to fall off this treadmill out of fear. "So, um, what was your name?"

"Apollo."

I laugh in his face. "That's not your name!!"

He smirks, "Is too."

"Nobody names their kids after Greek gods."

"Mine didn't."

"Did *not*?"

"Nope."

"Um, last time I checked, Apollo is the Greek god of the sun."

"He's also the god of archery and art. And music and poetry and just about everything else you can think of."

"How do you know that?"

He shrugs.

Okay, I must've woken up in an alternate universe this morning because guys this hot don't know anything about Greek mythology. I, on the other hand do, because I loved reading about mythology in school. Nothing made me happier than burying my nose in a book so I could read about all the fabulous goings-on of the gods and goddesses. So much juicy drama and intrigue, murder and mayhem. Yes, the gods are terrible people.

I shake my head, "So, if your parents didn't name you after the god Apollo, who did they name you after?"

"Have you ever seen Rocky?"

"Like, Rocky and Bullwinkle? The cartoon?"

He frowns, "No. The boxing movie. With Sylvester Stallone."

"Oh, I don't like violence. So no. Never seen it." I smile and he nods and stares into my eyes, which fuels my nerves. I need to think of another question quick. "What's your last name, if you don't mind me asking?"

"Armstrong."

"Apollo Armstrong? A.A.?" I grin, "I bet that means you were first in line all through school."

His face sours. "Something like that."

"Sorry. I didn't mean to…" I can tell I hit a nerve, but I have no idea why.

"Forget it."

"I'm sorry, I just…" *don't know what to say when I get this crazy nervous.*

"Don't worry about it." He tilts his head and gazes at me with his golden sunshine eyes. His eyes rival an actual sunrise.

I'm going to swoon.

Instead, I nearly trip and fall off the treadmill.

I struggle to regain my footing, white-knuckling the safety bar as I get my feet underneath me. I am such a klutz.

"You should slow that down a notch." He reaches over and presses beeping buttons until my treadmill slows down.

I'm blushing from the tips of my toenails to the ends of my long frizzy hair, which is currently pulled back in a thick ponytail. "Sorry."

"It's okay," he smiles.

I expect him to start laughing but he doesn't. His smile is genuine. That's proof that I'm in an alternate universe. Or I did die and go to heaven earlier and this is the after life. It's certainly good enough to be.

"I was gonna say that my dad named me after Apollo Creed, the villain in Rocky 1 and 2." He beams with excitement, obviously remembering the movie. "My dad and I must've watched that movie a million times when I was growing up. It's a classic. You should see it."

The look on his face makes me want to see it. And I never watch sports movies or sports anything. But I would watch nothing *but* sports if he was by my side. "I should," I smile. "It sounds interesting."

"Would you believe they're having a midnight screening of it Friday night at the Egyptian in Hollywood?"

I laugh, "No they aren't." I might have zero experience with men, but even I can detect something that's too good to be true.

He chuckles, "You're right. But I couldn't think of a good way to say I have all the Rocky movies on DVD and I watch them at my place all the time and you're invited if you ever want dinner and a movie."

Is he lying?

He must be lying.

The look on his face says he's not.

I swallow hard then mutter, "I would—"

WHAM!!

I fall face first on the treadmill and go shooting off the end like a slingshot. Thank goodness I'm covered in cushions. I tumble off the end and land on the rubber floor in a heap.

Apollo vaults off his treadmill like an Army Ranger jumping out of an airplane and kneels beside me. "Are you okay, Daphne?" His concern is obvious.

"I think I broke my face," I grimace, "and my boobs." I struggle to a sitting position and hold my face in my hands. People are staring, but I'm so distracted by Apollo, I barely notice.

"Let me see." He pulls my hands tenderly away.

He's touching me again.

I quiver.

"Is it broken?" I moan.

"What, your nose?"

"No," I giggle. "My whole face."

He chuckles and smiles at me, his eyes searching my features. "Nope. Everything looks perfect to me." His sunshine grin relaxes me. He really does have an amazing smile. And those golden eyes mesmerize.

And the way he says the word perfect in relation to me melts my heart.

He winks, "Now that you're all warmed up, I think it's time for you to get pumped."

That was innuendo! I heard it! I just got innuendoed by the hottest man on the planet!

Oh. My. Gosh.

I didn't realize heaven was *this* good.

Chapter 4

DAPHNE

"Are you sure we're allowed to do this? Here? It seems so…" I can't even finish my sentence but I want to say it seems so scandalous.

"I'm the trainer, Daphne. I think I know the rules," he says gruffly. "So do another squat."

"Right. Sorry." I feel stupid. I stand with my feet shoulder width apart and I have an empty weight bar on my shoulders. To me, it weighs a million pounds. I also feel stupid because I probably insulted him by questioning his authority. That's me: Daphne Bowman, S.H.W.

What does S.H.W. stand for?

Social Half-Wit.

It's my usual title when I'm around men I'm attracted to. I may be good at small talk at the office, but when I'm around hunky men?

S.H.W.

"Another squat," he barks. If he hadn't been so nice earlier, I would think he was being a demanding prick.

I squat down, my thighs trembling.

I'm sure you're wondering what's so scandalous about doing squats at a gym. Embarrassing, maybe, because a child could squat an empty weight bar. But me? I'm struggling and sweating after only five reps. Here's the scandalous part: there's a mirror in front of me. Every time I squat down, my knees go out. In layman's terms, I'm spreading my legs. Which means I can plainly see my hoo-ha in the mirror right in front of me. Well, it's covered by my lycra leggings. But I can see it. So can Apollo.

I swear he's staring.

Despite my extra long active Tee, which hangs below my waist, it bunches up every time I squat. In essence, I'm putting on a free show.

"Arch your back," he demands. "You have to stick your butt out. Do another one."

My eyes flash.

I'm entirely certain this kind of talk is completely inappropriate for a personal trainer. But none of the other gym members lifting weights around us seem to care. I can't say that I mind either.

I squat down again and this time, instead of staring at my crotch, he stares at my ass.

"Mmmm, just like that. Perfect."

I almost fall over laughing. That is most definitely not appropriate! But I'm all kinds of turned on. When I squat down yet again, the image of him lying naked on the floor beneath me with a rock hard cock explodes into my mind. My lady parts clench. I think it has something to do with the way the rest of me is clenching every time I do a squat. It's working *those* muscles. Yes, there's no doubt in my mind: doing squats is definitely scandalous.

And I'm loving every second of it.

I push up with my legs and start to wobble because my muscles are completely fatigued. "I'm gonna fall," I mutter, starting to panic.

"I'll spot you," he says. He comes up right behind me and squats down, matching my position. He is literally three inches behind me. I feel his body heat. "Two more."

"Are you sure?" I nearly gasp. His pelvis is right behind mine. If I were to suddenly sit down, I would sit right on his muscular lap. And we all know what's in men's laps.

"Yeah. Two more. You've got this. And I've got you."

He can have me any way he wants. I squeeze my legs hard and start to rise.

"That's it," he grunts. "One more. Go down."

I want *him* to go down. Maybe later. I bend my knees and my butt brushes across his black khakis.

Gulp.

He. Is. Hard.

No, not muscular. I figured that out earlier when I first laid eyes on him. I mean cock hard. There's a steel torpedo in his pants, or in this case, shorts. I would shoot straight up to standing because I'm so surprised, but my legs are too tired.

"All the way down," he grunts. "Go deep."

My knees buckle. There's no way I'm standing up after hearing those words. "I'm gonna fall!"

His arms come up from behind and hook under mine. "It's okay. I've got you. Go all the way down."

Okay, this has gone well beyond inappropriate. Or even scandalous. This is X-rated. But I go down anyway. When I get to the bottom, my legs are done. "I can't stand up," I whimper.

"I've got you." Instead of lifting me up with his arms through my armpits like I would expect, he pushes up with his pelvis.

Oh, that's it. That hit the spot. Literally.

All the strength goes out of my legs.

But he lifts me up anyway, pushing with that pelvis of his. If I wasn't so attracted to him, I would insist he stop. But I am, so I don't. I would like to insist he never stop, but I'm not that brave. He pushes me up to standing.

I gasp, breathless. "Was that one or two? I don't think I can do another one." I am really out of shape. Not that I ever was in shape.

"Do one more for me, Daphne."

Our eyes meet in the mirror in front of us.

Heat pours off him from behind me.

His hardness presses against the crack of my ass.

This is not only the sexiest thing I could possibly imagine, it's the first time anything genuinely sexy has ever happened to me. Ever. I've never even been on a date. And I certainly skipped prom and all that other high school foolishness.

"One more, Daphne. I'll help you."

I sit down suddenly, wanting desperately to have him inside me. I may have no experience with men or dating, but I know what sex is. I have fingers. I nearly moan out loud when I feel his hard heat.

We go down together.

"Watch your form in the mirror," he commands.

Speechless, I nod, my eyes locked on his. Form? What's he talking about? I can't stop looking into his gorgeous sunshine eyes.

We go down all the way to the bottom.

I am wide open. My legs *and* the other part.

He stares right at my center.

I swear, his gaze makes it burn.

"Do it," he mutters in my ear. "Squeeze your thighs and take the weight. This time it's all you." His soft cello tones make these by far the sexiest words ever said by a man to a woman.

"I can't," I wince. I really have no strength left. Whether because I'm so out of shape or because I'm overwhelmed by the sensuality of the moment, it doesn't matter.

"You can. I've got you. Squeeze as hard as you can."

I would like nothing more than to squeeze him as hard as I can. With my insides.

"Push, Daphne."

Oh, gawd. I clench my thighs as hard as I can. This time, everything inside me clenches too. I can barely do this. But I push and push and I start to rise.

"That's it. Push." His hips and thighs brush mine. "Push as hard as you can, Daphne. Push for me."

I do. And that's it. Warmth blooms through me and I have an orgasm. Not a huge one, but I know what one is and I just did. I came.

"Do it," he grunts softly in my ear. "Push hard."

Thank God I'm wearing these moisture wicking leggings *and* extra thick granny panties beneath because I'm soaked. I just hope it doesn't show because Apollo is staring straight at it. "I can't," I moan. This time I really can't. My legs are all out of gas.

His hips thrust into me and his arms pull me against his hard chest and he stands us both up. I'm essentially sitting on his erection. I never want to stand up again. I'll sit here forever while he fucks me through his khakis. I mean, if he's okay with that.

He lifts the bar up over my head, taking it from me. It's easy for him to get the bar over my head because he's so tall. He sets it on the metal rack in front of the mirror with a clang then immediately sits down on the edge of the rack, which is a waist-high horizontal metal beam.

That was weird. Why did he sit down so fast?

He folds his hands in his lap and smirks. "So, ahh... good job on those squats."

I stifle a giggle. *How cute. He's hiding his hard on.* "I'll say," I grin. "Is that, um, normal? I mean, for you to, um, spot me like that?" By "spot" I mean fuck.

He knows what I mean. He blushes. Yes, actually blushes. It's hard to tell because he has tan skin, but he's blushing. "Uh, yeah. Spotting is a safety precaution."

I almost say, *If you were taking safety precautions just now, you would've worn a condom.* But I don't. I just smile and giggle. "What's next?"

"Uh, why don't we take a minute to rest. You look like you need a minute to catch your breath."

"You look like you need a minute to—" *jerk off while I watch. Or fuck me.* I don't say anything, but I think he can read my thoughts because his blush intensifies and we lock eyes.

We both start snickering.

"You're dangerous," he chuckles.

"I'm dangerous?! You were the one who—!" I stop myself again. I can't believe we're having this moment.

But we are.

Like I said, heaven is a great place.

There is no other rational explanation for the amazing time I'm having with Apollo. I mean, he is the god of the sun, so it's only fitting that this is heaven.

Or Mount Olympus at the very least.

Chapter 5

DAPHNE

"Your seven o'clock is here," Fashion Forty Fiona says after walking up to where Apollo is watching me use one of the lat pull-down machines. I swear, he had me use it just so he could stare at my boobs while my arms go up and down.

I let the bar go all the way up and release it. The weights clank onto the stack. I fold my arms across my chest because I don't like the way Fashion Forty's eyes sweep over my body like she's judging me.

"Is it seven already?" Apollo asks, surprised.

"Yes," she says. "She's waiting downstairs."

"Oh, okay. Can you tell her I'll be right down?"

"Sure." She smiles at him coquettishly, "Maybe when you finish up later you can give me a personal training session too." She's flirting. It's obvious.

Despite all the scandalous squatting Apollo and I did together, I can't deny Fashion Forty's beauty. I expect Apollo to suddenly say, *Sure. I'll give you a personal training session, Fiona. It'll be better than the one I just gave this cow.*

He scratches the back of his head. "I think I've got appointments until late. I won't have time. Maybe next week? No, wait. Next week I'm booked solid. Yeah, I really don't think I'll have time for anything. Maybe you can get one of the other trainers to help you out?" He winks at me so that Fiona can't see it.

Fiona's eyes narrow. "I'll do that," she grumbles before walking away.

When she's gone, Apollo says, "Sorry about that."

"Oh, no. It's okay."

"I didn't mean her. I meant, sorry for losing track of time. I really should've paid closer attention to the clock."

"Oh, right." Why do I feel disappointed again?

"Next time, I'll make sure I do."

"Next time?"

He smiles sunshine, "Yeah. Next session. You get ten free training sessions. I mean, that is, if you want me as your trainer again?" He looks… bashful and uncertain of himself.

How in the world could he possibly think I would not want to do that again? I will go to the gym every day until forever if he's my spot-squatting trainer. "Of course! I mean, yes. That would be great. How do I make sure I'm on the schedule for next time? I mean, in case I miss the confirmation email?"

He smirks, "I'll remember."

"Great. Um, what day should we meet up?"

His eyes circle thoughtfully, "How about…"

I want to say, *How about tomorrow! How about in an hour when you finish with your next client? How about you forget your next client and we go back and do more squats?*

He pins me with his eyes. "I'm thinking you probably need a recovery day. We went at it pretty hard today."

I can go hard at it right now if you can. "Um, okay. So, Friday?"

"Let me check my schedule." He pulls his smart phone out of his pocket and thumbs the screen.

I notice the sun has gone down. The wall of windows in the gym is now a dark mirror reflecting the people on the machines inside. Despite the fact that I need to get home and eat and shower and get ready for bed before work tomorrow, I feel energized. Like I could do spot-squats all night long. *Allllll* night.

"Let's see… I'm booked from four until eight." He looks disappointed. "That's pretty late. I'm sure by eight you'll be out on a date with someone."

Okay, that's ridiculous because:

a) I've never been on a date, and

b) Is he serious?

After the squat fucking he gave me, how can he possibly think I would go out on a date with anyone other than him?

"Actually," I chuckle, "it just so happens I don't have any plans Friday night."

"Really," he says thoughtfully. His face lights up with his sunshine smile and it brightens the entire gym like the sun is still up.

Something about that smile sets me at ease. It's… comforting. I love that feeling. For once, I'm relaxed around a man I'm desperately attracted to. It makes me feel like…myself. Like I don't have to second guess everything I'm saying. It's wonderful. "Yeah," I laugh, "every other day *except* Friday I'm out on dates with tons of different guys. Friday is my rest day."

He frowns, looking confused. "That doesn't sound good."

"I'm kidding." I touch his wrist briefly.

Wow. I'm flirting. I can't believe I'm *actually* flirting. I don't think

I've ever flirted before. Well, I flirt with the male patients at work all the time, but only the ones over sixty. And that's just friendly flirting. This is sexy flirting and it's the real thing.

"Good," he says.

"Good what?"

"Good that you were kidding."

"About what?"

"All those dates." His eyes are suddenly dark. "With other dudes." He sounds almost... angry.

A thrill sweeps through me. What is happening? Is he going caveman on me? I'm going to faint again. "Actually, I don't really date much. I mean, hardly at all." In other words, never.

His sunshine returns like a summer morning. "Then I'll see you Friday at eight."

"At eight." I giggle.

"It's a date."

Chapter 6

APOLLO

After I finish with my last client that night, I head to the locker room to grab my gym bag.

Fiona passes me on the way. "Hey, Apollo! You done for the night?"

"Yeah. Gonna head home. It's been a long day."

She rolls her eyes. "I bet."

What's that supposed to mean? She doesn't know I was at the cemetery. She didn't mean Daphne, did she? I don't want to know.

She smiles, "I'm going out with some girlfriends later to get drinks and listen to music at Piano Bar. Do you want to meet us there?" She curls her lush lips and lowers her eyelids seductively.

There's no doubt that Fiona is gorgeous. She's my usual type: total knockout. We've had this flirtation thing going since the day I started working here a few months ago. I would've asked her out already, but then my dad died.

Tony, the manager, walks up right then. "Hey, Apollo. Fiona, can I talk to you in my office for a second?"

She smiles at him, "Sure." Then turns to me, "We'll be at Piano Bar. Come join us!"

I can't help but stare at her ass as she walks away. It's perfect and she knows it. You can tell from the way she bounces it on purpose.

I could go to Piano Bar and drink there instead of go home and drink by myself. That doesn't sound like fun. Maybe I'll head over to the bar. It's only a few blocks from here. And you never know who you're gonna see play at Piano Bar. I heard Katy Perry got started there.

When I walk into the locker room, I pull my gym bag out of my locker and the SMIRNOFF bottle clunks against the metal doorframe. I unzip the bag and pull it out.

I toss it in my hand and watch the vodka slosh around inside.

I smile to myself and shake my head.

Some old guy in a white gym towel walks by. "You put that in all the sports drinks you sell out front and you'll sell a lot more sports drinks." He grins.

"True that," I chuckle.

I walk into one of the bathroom stalls and pour the booze down the toilet. Flush.

After I walk out of the gym and take the stairs up to the roof of the parking garage, I stop and stare at the moon glowing overhead. I think about what that kid Owen said at the cemetery today.

I tip my head up to the stars and say, "You were listening to me bitch and moan at the cemetery today, weren't you? Did you send her?"

No answer.

I whisper, "Thanks, Dad."

DAPHNE

The next day.

"That is scandalous, Daphne!" my work friend Lynn gasps.

"I know, right?" I laugh.

"I'm sure he's not allowed to do that to the clients."

"That's what I said!"

We both laugh and nibble on our sandwiches.

We're having lunch in the courtyard outside the building where we both work in the Valley. Lynn is the receptionist slash administrative assistant for the chiropractor across the hall from the dentist's office where I work. We eat out here together every day it isn't raining, which in LA is nearly year round.

"I'm surprised he hasn't gotten fired with behavior like that," Lynn says.

"I certainly won't turn him in," I blush.

"You dirty girl! Do you think he does that with all the women?"

"I hope not!"

We both laugh like high school.

After we catch our breath, Lynn sighs, "Ooooh, Daphne, I wish I had your life. That is the steamiest story I think I've ever heard."

"Are you telling me Matt has never done anything that hot?"

Lynn levels a look at me and smirks. "Please. We've been married ten years. Matt has *never* squat fucked me. Not that I can remember."

"I think you'd remember." I giggle again. "Maybe you can convince him to try it sometime."

"With Dylan and Nicholas yammering away in the apartment? Uh-uh. Not gonna happen. There's no place for Matt and I to do it."

"Maybe you should join a gym and get your own hunky personal trainer," I say coyly.

She smirks, "Can I have yours?"

"No! No sharing!" I laugh. "Join another gym."

"I'm kidding. I don't think Matt would like the idea of me spending so much time up close and personal with a certified hunk." She swoons, "Oh, to be single again. Sometimes I miss all that wild and crazy fun. When do you see your hunk next?"

"Friday. I think we have a date."

Her eyes explode. "What?! Are you serious?"

"I think so."

"I guess he wasn't done squat fucking you!" She guffaws.

"Lynn! Shush!" I start to blush and glance around to make sure no one is close enough in the courtyard to listen in. Nope, the few people outside are busy chatting or reading.

Lynn wipes her fingers with a paper napkin. "Do you want to walk over to Starbucks? They have a new chocolate chip cookie dough cake pop I've been dying to try."

"Hmmm. I don't think so."

"Did your hunky personal trainer put you on a diet?"

"No, I did," I smile.

"Good for you, girl!" she cheers. "In that case, let's both go on a diet. I could stand to lose a few pounds myself. Ever since Nicholas started the first grade, I haven't had anyone to chase around."

"Maybe you and Matt need a date night. Send the boys off to their grandmother's so the two of you can take up sex squatting," I mutter.

"You have the dirtiest mind I've ever heard, girl!!" She howls with laughter. "But I like your style. So, what are you and Mr. Hunk going to do for your date?"

"I'm not entirely sure. He didn't say."

She narrows her eyes. "But he told you he wanted to take you out after your training session, right?"

"Ummm, sort of?"

"What *did* he say?" Now Lynn sounds concerned.

"He said, 'It's a date'."

"That's it? Just, 'it's a date'?"

I nod.

"Maybe he meant your training session."

"I don't know…" Now I'm getting worried.

"Did he mention anything about *after* your session?"

I close the lid on my Tupperware sandwich keeper with a pop and stare at it. "No."

"Be careful, Daphne." Her voice is full of compassion.

"I know," I sigh. "But we did the squat sex thing. Doesn't that mean he's interested?"

Lynn places a comforting hand on my knee. "I have no doubt the man is interested in sex with you. Any man would be. But that doesn't mean your gym hunk is interested in anything more."

"But he was so polite and we had so much fun talking and I thought…" I groan. "I don't know what I thought."

"Don't beat yourself up, Daphne. Some guys are very forward like that. And maybe he does like you like that. I don't know. I *hope* he likes you like that. I really do. I just… I don't want you getting hurt. You're my tender little flower," she grins.

I smile. She's been calling me that ever since I told her I was still a virgin. I smirk, "One of these days, I'd like to get rid of my tender little flower."

"Oh, Daphne, I'm sure you will. Whether it's Mr. Hunk at the gym or another man, you will. I promise."

"So, should I bring a change of clothes tomorrow when I go back to the gym? Just in case he really did mean a *date* date?"

Her eyes drift in thought and her brows knit. Then they relax into a smile. "Why not? What have you got to lose? The worst thing that can happen is that he squat fucks you and sends you home a wet and happy camper!"

We both burst into lurid laughter once again.

Chapter 7

"There she is," Apollo grins on Friday evening when I walk through the front doors of Body Fitness. Since it's nearly eight, the place is much quieter than last time. He leans against the reception desk. Fashion Forty Fiona is standing behind it. Were they just talking?

I don't care. Apollo is waiting for me, not her.

When I see his sunshine smile, I feel myself glow. I can't get over how much better I feel about myself when I'm around him. "Hey, Apollo."

He turns to Fiona and says, "We'll talk later. When I get off."

Fiona glances at me then says to him, "If you need any help *getting off*, let me know."

She did not just say that!

"Yeah." He grins his rugged grin. "Catch you later."

She purrs, "Have fun with…" Her eyes sweep over me in that judgmental way she has. "…*her*." Then she tips up her nose without actually acknowledging me and walks into HOG's office, which is empty.

Again? What is with her? And more importantly, why are she and Apollo talking about getting off together after my training session ends? What happened to our date?

I am such an idiot.

Lynn was right. When Apollo said "It's a date," it was just an expression. He obviously meant we had an appointment. I should've known better. I am so desperate it's shameful. I held onto hope when I should've let go.

Now I feel stupid because I've got a gigantic garment-sized duffel bag under my arm with a change of clothes for our supposed date later, and all he's holding is his clipboard. Like last time, I'm already wearing my gym clothes because I'm too shy to change in front of a bunch of strange women. But I was all geared up to change into my date clothes for our, groan, "date" later. Believing Apollo was going to take me out gave me the courage I needed. But now that I realize how foolish I was for assuming he meant an honest to goodness, two-people-attracted-to-each-other, date, I just want to run and hide.

"You ready to work out?" he asks. "Or are we just gonna stand here all night?"

Why does he have to say it like that? So... mean? I bite my lower lip and hold back tears. "Um, I need to put my gym bag back in my car." And a moment to collect myself before I decide whether or not to drive away and never come back. I am *so* embarrassed right now.

He nods. "Yeah, I don't think it'll fit in the gym lockers. It's pretty big." The look on his face says, *You're pretty big too. I don't know what I was thinking when I squat fucked you.*

I grimace. "I'll be right back."

He smiles, "I'll be right here."

Is he being polite? I think he's just being polite.

I barge out the doors and nearly knock over a guy coming inside. "Sorry!" I dash across the parking structure that is attached to the gym and lock myself in my car. Tears run down my cheeks and I smear them away.

I stick my key in the ignition.

I start to turn it.

No!

I'm not doing this! I'm not running away. It doesn't matter how foolish I've been. I came here to get in shape. Whether Apollo meant date or not isn't the issue. The issue is me.

Me.

Taking back my beauty.

Not for anyone else. For me.

It doesn't matter that Apollo was all over me last time. For all I know, he's a manwhore who steals feels from women all the time. I'm probably the sixtieth woman he's squat fucked this week. Just one more amusement for him.

So what?

I liked it.

And yes, if it *never* happens again, I'll miss it. But I enjoyed it and will always remember it fondly. Why? Because it was proof that I'm not so horrid that all men find me repulsive. So I'll hold on to my memory of Wednesday and do my best to get through today.

After, I can cry my eyes out over a bowl of ice cream, which I will regret, then come back here next week and do my very best to get in shape.

That is what I'm doing, whether or not Apollo ever gives me a second look.

I climb out of my car but I leave my duffel bag holding my date clothes on the front seat because I won't be needing the new dress I bought special for the occasion.

I march back into the gym.

DAPHNE

"Good job," Apollo says at the end of our hour long session. "You really nailed the squats this time."

By "nail" he doesn't mean anything sexual. There was no squat fucking. Not even legitimate squat spotting. Or boob staring from him while I did the lat pull down machine. It was oh so very platonic and proper. But I'm okay with that. I'm old enough to realize our little moment Wednesday was a one time thing. He probably already forgot it happened. That's okay. It really is.

He looks at his watch. "Well, it's nine. I promised Fiona I'd talk to her."

"You do that," I smirk. I can't wait to get home so I can shower and slip into that bowl of ice cream. I turn to go.

"I only need about ten minutes," he says.

Cellos.

I stop and turn around. "What?"

"I need to talk to Fiona real quick. One of the trainers quit today so we have to juggle everyone's schedule around for next week. I have to pick up a few extra shifts." He smiles sunshine.

"Oh." I wasn't expecting that. "Okay. Well, I should probably go. Maybe I'll see you next week?"

He scratches the back of his head nervously. "About that..." Now he's going to tell me this is the last time he's ever going to coach me.

I brace myself for imminent disappointment.

He smirks, "Uhh, I was wondering. I know it's kind of last minute, and I probably should've asked you this Wednesday, but would you want to go grab a bite to eat with me?"

Did I hear him right?

The puppy dog look on his face says I did.

I blurt, "What, like now?!?"

"Yes now. I haven't eaten in hours and I'm starving."

YES YES YES!!! I don't jump up and down despite my desire. "That sounds... nice." I sound very demure.

His smile lights up. "Really?"

I grin, "Yes, really."

"Awesome! As soon as I finish with Fiona, I'll go change and we can get out of here. I know the perfect place on Melrose."

"Oh? Where?"

"ReaXion. Do you know it?"

"I've heard of it, but I've never been."

"You'll love it."

He said love!

"I'll keep it short with Fiona then we'll go." We walk up to the front reception area together. He stops, "Wait, are you leaving?" He sounds disappointed.

"I just need to get something from my car. Real quick. I'll be right back."

"Oh, okay," he says, relieved.

As soon as I walk casually through the front doors into the parking garage, I sprint to my car and grab my gym bag. Then I sprint back to the doors and stop to catch my breath before opening them. My heart is beating a thousand miles an hour, and not because of sprinting.

It's a real official date!

When I go inside, Apollo is talking to Fiona behind the counter. He glances at me, "Almost done. I'll need two minutes to change."

"No rush," I smile.

Fashion Forty Fiona glares at me.

Fuck you, bitch!

I prance into the women's locker room with a giant smile on my face. Although the locker room is empty, and the showers have individual stalls with shower curtains, I don't think I'm comfortable showering in such a public place. Maybe some other time. I didn't sweat that much. I've never been a sweater. Then again, I've never exercised, so maybe I should shower? No. I don't have time and I don't have a towel or soap or anything.

A real date!

I can't believe this is happening.

I tear my gym clothes off with shaky hands. I manage to drop everything onto the tile floor at one point or another. I throw on deodorant, a little eyeliner which I rarely wear, and some neutral lip gloss which I never wear, and call it good. My giant frizz of curly hair is back in a ponytail like always. I never wear it down because it's too dangerous. It's always in my face and never behaves and nine times out of ten I'm having a bad hair day.

But you know what?

I'm about to go on a date!

With Mr. Cello himself, certified Hot Hunk Apollo Armstrong.

I'm going on a date!!!!
My very first!!!!

So I'm letting my hair down, ladies! I peel the thick hair tie (I use the ones as big as bridge cables) out of my hair and shake it out. It's a gigantic smokey ball of hair. Then I climb into my new dress and stuff my workout clothes into my duffel and slide my feet into my strappy 3 inch sandals. On my way out of the locker room, I stop in front of a full length mirror. I primp my hair and call it good. It really needs a hedge trimmer, but at least it has plenty of body and bounce.

Okay this is it.

Now or never.

I walk through the gym to look for Apollo.

At this late hour, the place is essentially empty.

I guess Apollo is probably waiting for me at the front door? I walk up to the reception area.

Fashion Forty is at the desk but Apollo isn't. She rolls her eyes at me.

"Ummm, did Apollo leave?"

She shrugs and turns her back to me.

Why is she so horrid?

I wait a few more minutes.

No Apollo.

Now I'm getting nervous. Did he leave?

Was this all a big prank staged by him and Fiona to break my heart? He wouldn't do that, would he? She would. But would he? My face heats. I hope he wouldn't.

Fiona smirks at me.

I can't stand here with her staring at me. I consider putting my giant duffel bag in my car because I want Apollo to see me in my dress, not me hiding behind my giant bag. But if I go and do that, he may wonder where I went. He did say he was going to change. Maybe he's still changing. So I walk back toward the locker rooms.

And wait.

Gosh, this isn't going to backfire on me, is it?

The cellos play: "Sorry about that," Apollo says.

Relief washes over me. I turn expecting to see him in his purple polo and black khakis. Nope. He's wearing a stylish steel gray V-neck sweater with black accents. It's glued to his chest and shoulders and I can make out every muscle. Black jeans cling to his muscled legs and black dress shoes complete the look.

He is stunning.

I giggle, "You clean up nice."

"So do you." His smile rises like the morning sun. "Nice dress."

"I wore it because you liked blue."

He grins, "Yeah I do. Especially on you." His eyes slide up and down my color block dress.

The middle panel is of course blue, and the outside panels with the cap sleeves are black. The woman at Lane Bryant said it was slimming and based on the look on Apollo's face, it's working its magic. I've never had a guy look at me with so much naked desire. The square neck of the dress doesn't show cleavage, but Apollo is acting like it does.

After he finishes staring, he smiles, "Sorry I took so long. I hopped in the shower real quick because I've been here all day surrounded by sweat."

"Awww, you didn't have to do that."

"Are you kidding? I totally did. For you."

I am both flattered and freaked. "Um, I didn't shower. Maybe I should? I can shower really fast, I promise!" Panic sets in because he smells incredible. I can't tell if it's just him or his cologne, but he smells like M.A.N. The kind who wrestles crocodiles with one hand or fights tigers with a threatening look that says, *Settle down, Stripes. I'm the king of this here jungle.*

I probably smell like a dirty kitchen mop.

He steps right up to me and leans down. His face is inches from my naked neck. He inhales slowly.

I wince, expecting him to gag. Not that I stink, but I didn't shower and he did.

In his dirtiest Cello voice (played on the low and manly C string, the thickest fattest deepest one) he says, "You smell like sex to me. Don't shower. I want to smell you all night. Just like this."

"Ummm…" Goosebumps!! We're talking my entire population of skin geese flying south for the winter! And by south, I mean the whole flock of them is migrating straight down to *my* south because my panties just became a tropical paradise. Think hot and humid and sinfully sultry like nobody's business.

Now I really do need a shower. Or at the very least a change of panties.

Somebody grab a bucket!

Chapter 8

DAPHNE

Unlike the gym, ReaXion on Melrose is packed with people and loud. We can't even get a table. The hostess tells us the wait is two hours.

"I didn't realize it would be this crowded." Apollo sighs and turns to me, "Do you want to eat at the bar? We might be able to find a table in there."

"Okay." I'm suddenly nervous that we won't find one and he'll say, *Oh well. Maybe next time.* But there won't be a next time.

He leads me into a crowded room that is louder than the restaurant section. The bar is all dark wood and straight lines mixed with rough-hewn rock walls. Softly glowing lights like starbursts hang from the ceiling at random intervals and at random heights. It's beautiful.

It turns out that walking in 3 inch heels is not my forte. But I do my best. Which means I wobble. I'm used to flats. "Oops!" I nearly twist my ankle.

"I've got you," Apollo says, wrapping a strong arm around my waist.

"You saved me," I joke sarcastically because having his arm on my waist is so overwhelming I can't even deal with it. So I joke.

"Yeah I did," he smiles down at me.

"How tall are you, anyway?"

"Six four."

"Geez. You're way taller than me."

He glances at my boobs. "Great view too."

"Apollo!"

He chuckles. "Let's find a table." Luckily, a tall bar table in the far corner is open. "Is this okay?"

"Perfect." It's perfect because I can't help but notice that nearly every woman in the bar here at ReaXion is staring at Apollo. So are many of the men. We're pretty close to West Hollywood, after all. I'm more than happy to take a table in the corner so we can get away from prying eyes.

He pulls a barstool out for me and I sit. He literally lifts me *and* the stool up and scoots me up to the table.

"Oh!" I blurt. "How strong are you?"

"Strong enough," he smirks as he sits down.

We start talking immediately. Our conversation flows naturally and is just as much fun as it was on Wednesday. This is the Apollo I know and, um, enjoy. Really, *really* enjoy. One might say I *lenjoy* him. Lenjoy with an L.

After a while, he looks around the frantic bar. "Where's our waitress? It's been a half hour since we sat down."

"Oh, I'm okay." I really am. Being with Apollo makes everything okay. I'm not even hungry after working out, which is good. The less calories the better.

"You need food. I need food. Or at least water. Can't have you getting dehydrated. Or passing out from low blood sugar after a workout." He pushes out his stool. "What do you want from the bar?"

"Water is fine." I'm sure he's right about the low blood sugar thing, so I don't want to get my calories from alcohol or a soda. I know *that* much about nutrition.

"Okay. Two waters. I'll be right back."

While I wait, I scan the restaurant. I can't get over how beautiful everyone is here at ReaXion. People aren't nearly as attractive up in Van Nuys where I work, and that's only a few miles from here. But we are near the heart of Hollywood. It's somewhat intimidating. I remind myself that I look good in my dress. And I feel good.

That's what counts.

"Hey," a strange male voice says.

I turn to see a cute blond guy in a black blazer slow to a stop beside my table.

"Hi," I say shyly. I'm not used to guys talking to me in bars. In fact, it never happens. Mainly because I don't go to bars. Ever.

"You're not here alone, are you?"

"Oh, no. I'm with..." I almost say, *my date*. But I don't because I'm suddenly uncertain. This guy is making me nervous. Or something. "... a friend."

Cute guy's smile widens. "That's good, because I was gonna say a woman like you shouldn't be out on a Friday night by herself."

"Like me? What's that supposed to mean?" I instantly assume the worst.

His eyes flash, "Whadda you mean, *like you*? You're gorgeous."

Is he joking? He must be joking. Nobody calls me gorgeous.

He offers his hand, "I'm Seth."

I shake his hand gingerly. "I'm Daphne."

"Nice name. Mind if I join you?" He motions to Apollo's empty stool.

"Oh, ummm…"

"Your friend. Right. That's cool. So, uhh, do you come here often?" He winces. "That was stupid. I'm sorry, I'm never good with pickup lines."

Pickup lines? I can't believe this is happening to me. Seth is hitting on me! I giggle nervously, "Me neither. Just pretend we know each other."

"Huh?"

I laugh, "How's work, Seth? Still working those late hours?" I can't believe I'm flirting back.

"Right," he grins. "Late hours. Yeah, work is a bitch. The boss has been busting my ass all week." His eyes flash again as he laughs.

This is surreal. "I hate those ass-busters," I giggle.

"Aren't they the worst?" He chuckles.

Our eyes lock.

Seth is interested.

In me.

I know it like I know my own name. What I don't know is how this could possibly be happening to me. I have never had a guy walk up to me in a bar or even a bus station and ask me anything other than if I will give him money. This is the polar opposite of that. Seth is asking for my affection. Before this week, no man had ever asked me for that.

He rests his hand on the back of my bar stool. "So, um, what else?" His fingers brush my arm and I nearly jump.

Did he do that on purpose? "Uhhh," I laugh, not sure what to say. But I do know that Seth is the kind of cute I should be dating. Not ravishing like Apollo, but realistic. If I'm being honest, this thing with Apollo is a fluke. A statistical anomaly. Sooner or later, reality is going to set in and he's going to realize I'm not Fashion Forty Fiona or whoever else he's used to dating. If I'm being sensible, I should give Seth my phone number so he can call me down the road when Apollo moves on to someone more suitable.

"So…" Seth says, "Do you live near here?"

"I'm in the Valley."

"Me too!" Seth beams. "Where?"

"Van Nuys."

"I'm in Valley Glen! You're right next to me," he says, hope shining in his eyes. "I bet we've crossed paths at some place like Trader Joe's without even knowing it."

"You shop at Trader Joe's?!"

He nods, grinning.

"I shop at Trader Joe's!!"

"Wow, small world," he chuckles, blushing.

He's blushing. For me.

"Hey, buddy," Apollo says, coming up behind Seth holding two big glasses of water with lemon wedges. He leans between me and Seth, forcing Seth to withdraw his hand from my barstool, and sets the glasses down.

Seth says, "You must be the friend."

Apollo shoots me a look. He looks mad.

Why? I don't know. But I wince anyway.

Apollo says to Seth, "I'm the *date*."

Seth's eyes go big. "Oh! Sorry! I was picturing someone more feminine!"

Apollo's sunshine smile slides into a delicious smirk. "What about me says feminine, buddy?"

"Sorry, I meant, you know, Daphne here said 'friend' so I thought she meant a girlfriend."

"Nope. She meant me. Her… *date*." He puts his arm around my shoulder.

Did Apollo just claim me? I believe he did.

Seth looks between me and Apollo. "Well, uhhh, it was nice meeting you, Daphne. Have fun."

"You too," I smile.

Seth scampers off toward the men's room.

A tiny voice in the corner of my heart says, *Shouldn't I have gotten Seth's number?*

I ignore it.

DAPHNE

"You know what I like about you?" Apollo says.

I nearly drop my fork in my chicken salad. I quickly set it down before I do. "Um, no. What?"

The bar is still crowded. Earlier, Apollo had to hunt down menus for us and order our food at the bar. He saws into his steak. "You're straight up. Nothing about you is fake."

"Thanks." It's true. I've always been honest and direct. What you see is what you get.

"You know what else I like about you?"

"What?"

"Your eyes. They're like blue diamonds."

"Do they even have blue diamonds?"

"Lucky Charms do."

I giggle, "Those are marshmallows in a kid's breakfast cereal. Not real diamonds."

"So? If they don't have them, they should make them."

"Why?"

"Because I have no doubt that anyone who sees your eyes never forgets them. And we all know that a memory is never as good as the real thing. I bet there's tons of people who, after looking into your eyes, want to immortalize the feeling your eyes gave them. If they had a pair of blue diamonds set into a ring, they could gaze upon those two blue diamonds every day. It wouldn't be as good as looking into your eyes, but it would help them better remember forever."

My jaw hangs open. "How do you know how to talk like this?"

He shrugs. "I don't know. But it's true. Your eyes are blue diamonds."

I roll my eyes, hiding my embarrassment. I can't even answer. Nobody has ever complimented me this much. Well, maybe my music teacher Mr. Atkins in high school, but that was for playing the cello. This is different.

Apollo says, "You know what else I like about you?"

"What?" I chuckle.

"You don't let your beauty turn you into a bitch."

"Are you drunk?" I laugh.

"Huh?"

I wring my napkin in my lap. It takes me a moment to figure out what I want to say. "Apollo, I'm not beautiful like Fiona or ninety percent of the other women I've seen at Body Fitness. You don't have to lie to me."

"I'm not lying," he says defensively.

"I'm serious, Apollo. You don't have to say all these things. It's... it's kind of weirding me out."

He frowns and sets his utensils down. He reaches over into my lap and takes my hand. "I'm not bullshitting you, Daphne. I think you're gorgeous."

"I'm fat, Apollo."

"You're healthy."

"That's not what my doctor says." I don't like where this conversation is going.

"Fine. That's why you came to me. To get into shape. I'm all about exercise and healthy living. I'm the perfect guy for you. Right?"

Now I'm distressed. "Why are you doing this, Apollo?"

"Doing what?"

"This. Me. You're out of my league."

"Have you looked in a mirror lately?"

Why does it feel like we're arguing? "Yes. After I put this dress on at the gym."

He shakes his head, "And did you not see what I saw when you walked out of the locker room just now? I'm pretty sure it was the same exact thing because the women's locker room doesn't have those bendy circus mirrors to make you look different."

"How do you know?" I chuckle.

"Because I've cleaned them."

"Oh."

He squeezes my hand again. "I don't know what's going on in that beautiful head of yours, but I can tell you that I've never had to prove to a woman I was attracted to her. Usually it's obvious and they figure it out. But with you, it's like you think I'm faking or something."

"Aren't you?" Whoops. I don't know why I said that.

He frowns. "No, I'm not fucking faking. What the fuck, Daph? What do I have to do to prove it to you?" He stands up suddenly.

He called me Daph. Swoon.

He wads his napkin and tosses it onto the table before walking off.

I am so utterly confused right now I just sit there as I watch him disappear into the crowd.

He probably just disappeared forever.

Maybe I should go look for Seth.

Chapter 9

"Can we talk?" I mutter.

Apollo stands outside in a service hallway that has a trellis roof. The hallway leads to the alley behind ReaXion. He stares up at the moon through the trellis, hands stuffed in his pockets, leaning against the stucco wall in a corner near a stucco planter that holds several small banana trees. He doesn't look at me.

I sigh. "I'm sorry, Apollo. It's just... You have to understand. This is all so new and overwhelming to me. I've never been on a date before. I mean, not a real date. Like this. With a guy like you. I'm not making any sense."

He nods but doesn't look at me. Just stares at the moon.

"Apollo? Can you at least look at me?"

"No," he grunts.

"Why not?"

He grumbles, "Because if I do, I'm going to kiss you."

Someone grab me a fainting couch. When none appears, I reach out and touch the back of his hand with my fingers.

His face swivels around, his brow dark, his eyes hot. He inhales deeply, scowling.

Then he throws me against the wall and buries his tongue in my mouth. I dig my fingers into his back muscles through his sweater and moan into his mouth.

Our tongues fight.

Our lips slip and slide.

A heat wave fires in my chest.

His hard hands grab my ass and he lifts me up, pushing my back against the wall and my thighs apart. My dress bunches up to my waist. I feel him hard between my legs. I wrap myself around him and he grinds against my wetness.

I moan again.

"Whoops!" a woman's voice says. "I think the ladies room is the other way!"

Apollo doesn't even notice.

He just attacks me with his lips and tongue. His hands massage my ass through my dress. I swear, he's going to make me come.

"Oh, Apollo…" I moan.

He breaks our kiss and leans his forehead against mine and growls, "Do you believe me now?"

"Kiss me," I whisper.

He does.

DAPHNE

"You know what I really like about you?"

This time, his question doesn't make me nervous but I can't manage to answer. My head is still spinning from our kiss. And that was three hours ago.

We stand beside his car, which is parked on a neighborhood side street near ReaXion. They kicked us out when they closed at 2am. I'm very aware of my lips. They're throbbing from all the kissing we did in that hallway outside under the light of the moon. It took at least a half an hour before the manager asked us to stop. I was so embarrassed. But we went back to our bar table to finish eating and talking.

Three hours later, they kicked us out at closing, and three hours later I can still feel the ghost of his cock pressing between my legs like a wet memory, fighting to punch through my underwear. I wish it was his real cock.

"Where'd you go?" he asks.

"I'm right here." I shiver pleasantly despite the warm evening.

He automatically puts his arm around me. "I was saying, you know what I really like about you?"

"What?" I'm all smiles.

"The way you make me feel."

"What do you mean?"

"You make me feel like life isn't running out."

I wrinkle my nose, "What does that mean?"

He stares at his dress shoes. "I don't normally talk about this, but with you, I feel like I can talk about anything."

"You can," I encourage.

He nods and meets my eyes. "My dad died last year at 52. On Christmas Eve."

"That's so sad, Apollo. I'm so sorry."

"Thanks. It was a sudden heart attack. Nobody saw it coming. The thing is, I'm 28. Over half way to the grave. There's nothing like seeing your own name staring back at you from a tombstone. It puts everything in perspective."

"Don't say that."

"I'm just being realistic. I miss that guy like you wouldn't believe. My mom misses him too. They had a great relationship. Really loved each other, you know? She was crushed when he died. I always envied what she had with him. I don't know anybody who has a relationship like my parents did. They were best friends."

"They were lucky."

"I know. But you know what?"

"What?"

"Something about you makes me feel like maybe I can find that special best friend connection with someone. Maybe some day." His eyes search mine. "Maybe even with you." He breaks eye contact and stares at his shoes.

As he says these things to me, I'm jumping up and down inside screaming, *I make a great best friend! Ask all my friends! They love me! I'm always there for them, helping them, making them laugh! I'm the bestest best friend anyone ever had! I'll totally be your best friend, Apollo! And you can screw me any time you want! Any time!* What I say is, "I know what you mean."

"You do?" He looks up at me, surprised.

"I mean, yeah. Who doesn't want that? Love and friendship and everything else." Everything being sex and babies, neither of which I've ever had, both of which I desperately want. With him. I know it's crazy. I've known him for two days. I can imagine Lynn telling me to be careful. To which I would say, *I'm 29. I only get older from here.* Common sense tells me I will never have another Apollo come along in my life. Ever.

He smiles, "We should go."

I'll go wherever fate takes us! "Yeah."

"We still need to get you back to your car at the parking garage." He beeps the alarm on his car and opens the passenger door for me. "Shall I help you into your carriage, madam?" His British accent is quite good.

Mine isn't, but I try anyway, "Why yes of course, good sir." I giggle as I climb into the car and he closes my door for me.

Chapter 10

APOLLO

Saturday morning.

"I met someone, Mom," I say to her across the table.

"What else is new," she laughs. "If I remember correctly, you meet a new woman every week."

"No I don't," I chuckle. "It's every day."

She shakes her head, "I can't believe you're my son. You're more incorrigible now than you were at sixteen."

"Yup," I laugh.

We're having brunch at the Hotel Del Coronado in San Diego. We sit at an umbrella covered table on the Sheerwater Restaurant patio. Just past the green grass and the brick path, the waves of the Pacific roll up onto the golden sand of the beach which runs along the west side of the hotel.

"Your father was never a wildcat like you." Her smile fades to sadness. "I miss your father." She stares at me with wet eyes.

"Me too." I choke out the words.

We both stare at the ocean for a long time.

"This was your father's favorite place to take me." Her words are thin and whispery.

"I know. He always told me if I was ever going to propose to someone, I should do it here."

Mom stares at me sideways, "Are you thinking about proposing to this new girl?"

"This one is special."

"How many times have I heard that before?"

I roll my eyes. She knows my history. "I'm serious, Mom. She's not like any of the other girls I've ever been with. She's one of my clients."

"Is that a good idea? Mixing business with pleasure?" She's always trying to mother me.

"It's fine, Mom. I'm not crossing any lines."

She arches an eyebrow.

"Okay. Maybe one line. But that's all I'm going to cross. I promise."

"And does this one have a name?"

"Yeah," I grin. "Daphne Bowman."

<<<<<<<>>>>>>>
DAPHNE

"How are things with Apollo?" Lynn asks over lunch in the courtyard several weeks later. "Still hot and heavy?"

"I wouldn't say that. But things are definitely perfect," I grin.

"Have you advanced the physical relationship?" She winks over her sandwich.

"Sadly, no. Another trainer quit two weeks ago, so Apollo had to pick up the slack."

"Are you two still having dinner after every training session?"

"Yup," I smile.

"Any more of those steamy after-dinner make out sessions?"

"No," I giggle. "I think he's tired from working so many hours. But I don't mind. Things started off a bit too quickly. I'm good at this pace."

"He's not pressuring you for sex?"

"Nope. But I think we're generally heading in a bedroom direction."

Lynn's eyes blow up. "My tender little flower! Are you going to let him punch your V-Card?"

I blush, "Probably. Did I tell you I'm a year older than him?"

"No! Younger men are always hot!"

"It's only a year."

"Still. I can't tell you how happy I am for you, Daphne. He sounds like a really great guy."

"He is."

"Any more squat fucking?" she chuckles over her sandwich.

"No! Mmmm, not yet, anyway."

"You know you want to try it for real. Without clothes."

"Lynn!"

"I would!"

"Is Matt still not into it?"

"Are you kidding? I never told him! He'd never stop pestering me if I had. Ever since having the boys, I don't think I have the energy for something like that. Matt and I are strictly missionary these days. So you better get any squat fucking done before you get married. That way you can fill me in on what I'm missing."

I roll my eyes. "I'll keep you posted."

"Do that." She chews on her sandwich and swallows while staring at me. "Is it just me, or are you losing weight?"

"I think I am. All of my clothes feel loose for the first time since I can remember."

"Well, good on you, girl! Take me with you when you go wardrobe shopping. I need some me time. Preferably with someone fun like you." She shakes her head, "I swear, my boys are driving me crazy. Dylan got in another fight at school."

"He did?! What happened?!"

"Oh, get this…"

Chapter 11

DAPHNE

Apollo says, "My mom's in town this weekend. Do you want to meet her?"

I do a squat. "Sure." The bar on my shoulders has a 25 pound plate on each side. My form is good: back arched, butt out.

Apollo doesn't even have to spot me. But he stares at my crotch in the mirror every time I go down. He bites his lower lip, "I really like how that looks."

I almost blurt, *Why don't you get under me then?* I don't. But I want to. It's been months since we met. Over ten official dress up dates. More if you count all the casual dinners we've shared. We're up into the thirties at this point. I know the old school rule is sex on the third date. After thirty dates, I think it's safe to say I should be ready. And considering I turn 30 in a few months, it's probably about time I lose my virginity. But Apollo still hasn't made a move. I lock eyes with him in the mirror. "You like this?"

"Yeah," he smirks.

I squat as low as I can. "Phew! This bar sure is heavy," I lie. It was way back on my first day here, but not anymore. I can squat it easily. "Gosh, I don't know if I can lift it all the way…" Do I sound like a damsel in distress? I hover near the bottom of my squat, my thighs quivering, my sex clenching. Working out with Apollo ogling me always turns me on. "I might need your… *help*. Do you think you can… *spot* me?"

"Sure," he smiles and squats behind me. "Do you need me to give you any help to start?"

"Yeah, give it to me good," I flirt.

"You can do it. You're only at ten reps. I've seen you do twenty easy."

I bump my butt against his crotch.

He doesn't seem hard.

What happened to his hard on? I miss it. The last time I felt it was at our first dinner date at ReaXion. Has it been that long? Months? I mutter, "Is something wrong?"

"I'm good. Are you good? Do you need me to take the weight?"

"I need you to take me!" I hiss.

Our eyes meet in the mirror.

He looks surprised.

That's odd.

"What's wrong, Apollo?"

He whispers, "There are people around!"

"So? That didn't stop you the first time."

"That was different. I didn't know you then. Now I... I don't want anyone looking at you. Like that."

"Like what?"

He continues whispering, "Like all sexy and turned on. Look around! This is a weight room. It's filled with dudes who are constantly checking out every woman in tight lycra. Including you."

How does he manage to always make me feel like a super model? He really is perfect.

My thighs are really shaking now. I try to press up to standing, but I can't. "Help! I can't lift it!"

He instantly hooks his arms under mine and we stand together. He takes the bar off my shoulders, pressing it over his head and mine like always, and sets it on the rack. "You okay?"

"Yeah," I exhale. "Fine." I grin at him, "Maybe if you don't want people looking, you should invite me someplace private instead of yet another restaurant."

"Okay. How about tonight I cook you dinner at my place?"

I thought he'd never ask.

DAPHNE

Keys jingle in the door lock of Apollo's apartment as he opens it for me. "Inside. Quick. I don't want to let the cat out."

I shuffle into the dark apartment. "You have a cat?"

He closes the door behind us and flips on the light in the small but surprisingly clean living room.

"I have to meet your cat," I grin, looking around the room.

He groans, "Don't tell me you're a cat lady."

"No. Not yet. I was hoping you could save me from that." I wink back.

"You picked the wrong guy."

"Why? Because you have cats?"

"Just one. He'll come out when he's ready. Have a seat." He motions toward the black leather couch. It's very masculine like the rest of his furniture. "Can I get you anything to drink?"

"Water's fine." I don't think I've drunk a single soda since I met Apollo. That's a record for me.

"That's my girl."

While he pours water from a pitcher in the kitchen, I glance around his intimate living room. "You don't have a TV."

"Nope."

"How do you watch movies?"

"On my laptop."

"But no TV?"

"Nope. I prefer books anyway." He nods to the right.

I twist behind me and see a bookcase packed full. I stand up and examine the spines. "Shut up! You have every Harry Potter book! And the Chronicles of Narnia! Crime and Punishment?! I haven't even read that. Sense and Sensibility? Have you read all these or are they just props?"

He chuckles as he hands me a glass of water. "Yeah, I've read them."

"But you… you're…"

"What?"

"Guys like you don't read Young Adult novels or classic literature."

"Really?" he sounds genuinely surprised. "Shit. What was I thinking?" He winks at me. "Drink your ice water. Before your brain melts."

I take a sip and sit down on the couch. "I absolutely love Harry Potter. What about Lord of the Rings?"

"Didn't read it but I saw the movies. They got kind of boring by the last Hobbit."

"You saw the movies?!?! WTF, Apollo! Where have you been all my life?!" I laugh.

"Right here."

"We could've gone to the Hobbit movies together! I went by myself because my friends have kids who are too young."

"Sorry. Maybe we can go see the next Star Wars together when it comes out. Or see The Force Awakens again. You have seen it, right?"

I stare at him. "Are you real?"

He flicks his big finger against my arm.

"Ow!" I rub it.

"I'm real."

"That was a rhetorical question."

"No it wasn't," he laughs. "You were really doubting yourself there for a minute."

That he knows what rhetorical means is the icing on the cake of his perfection. I'm still rubbing my arm, "You have hard fingers."

"That's not the only part of me that's hard," he grins.

I giggle nervously. We're all alone in his apartment. This might be the moment I lose my virginity.

"There he is," Apollo purrs as he reaches over the side of the couch. He picks up the fluffiest golden-eyed brown Maine Coon kitty I've ever seen. It starts purring immediately and curls into his arms.

"Oh my gosh! That is the cutest cat ever!"

"Not so loud. He already has a huge ego."

I grin as I reach out to scratch the cat's head. It's eyes close and it nuzzles up against my fingers. I'm good with cats.

Apollo lifts one of its paws and waves it at me. "Say hello to Daphne, Stink Foot." He says it as if he just called his cat Sweetie or something reasonably normal.

I raise my eyebrows a mile high. "Ummmm… is your cat really named Stink Foot?"

"It was either that or Shit Foot. Or Poop Foot. It took a while to decide. But I think he likes Stink Foot best."

"And why on earth do you call him that?"

"Because when he uses his box, he steps in his own turds."

"Don't you clean his box?"

"Yeah. Every day. Twice a day. But he always manages to step in it. So he's always tracking it around the apartment and I'm always cleaning it up."

Either that's the sweetest thing I've ever heard from a man or the most disgusting. I grimace, "How do you possibly put up with that?" I look around the apartment, expecting to see little brown cat paw prints everywhere.

"He only does it once in a while, but after the first time he did it, I dubbed him Stink Foot." He shrugs, "Love makes you do crazy things."

"Wait, did you just say you loved your cat?"

He smirks, "It's not like that makes me gay. It just means I like pussy," he winks.

"You did not just say *any* of that," I laugh.

"It's all true. I'm not gay, not that there's anything wrong with that, and I like pussy. Both kinds. The smelly kind and the furry kind."

"Wait, wait, wait." I plant my fists on my hips and glare at him. "Which kind is the furry kind and which is the smelly kind?"

"That depends."

"Depends on what?"

He grins, "Depends on what kind you have."

My eyes pop. "What? Me?"

"Yeah, you. Hairy or shaved?"

"What?! I'm not talking about my kitty cat!"

"Why not? We're talking about mine."

"But he's a cat! Mine is—"

"Hairy."

"Shut up!" I slap his arm. "Ow!"

"That's supposed to be my line," he smirks.

"Are you made of granite?"

"Back to the question. Shaved or hairy?"

"Would you stop asking that?! And stop saying hairy! It's grossing me out!"

"Furry?"

"That's worse! It reminds me of those animal costume fetish people! The ones who dress up like animals before having sex!"

"Are you into that?" he asks casually. "It's okay if you are."

"No! Are you?!"

"I'm into anything that involves you. The furrier the better."

"Stop!" I laugh.

"I'll stop when you answer my question. Furry or shaved?"

"Furry, all right! Now would you stop asking already!!"

"Now we can proceed."

"What?" I'm completely confused.

"I was going to say, regarding our little pal Stink Foot here—" he lifts the cat's front paws and the cat just purrs, "—considering you've got fur—" he winks at me, "—which I love by the way, and I call my cat Stink Foot, I think it's pretty obvious."

I shake my head, "Wait. What was pretty obvious? I'm completely lost."

"Your pussy is the furry kind I love, and I love my smelly furry cat Stink Foot." Apollo grins from ear to ear.

I scrutinize his face. "That better all be true. Or not true. Whichever isn't offensive. Because I can't figure out which is which." I shake my head and wrinkle my nose, "You are making me crazy!" I laugh.

He chuckles, "It's all true. And you're in good company because I'm crazy too." He turns to his cat. "Isn't that right, Stink Foot?"

The cat purrs and tips his head back against Apollo's chest, causing his little mouth to open and his purr to come out louder.

I wince, "Is his name really Stink Foot?"

"No. When I adopted him, they told me it was Stanley."

"You adopted Stanley?" I coo.

"Yeah. From the Humane Society. But call him Stink Foot. He likes it better than Stanley."

I frown, "I don't see how that's possible."

"That's because you're not named Stanley," he chuckles.

I nod thoughtfully, "Good point."

Apollo leans his head down and cradles the cat higher. Stink Foot, who I will call Stanley for my own sanity, stretches his neck up and kisses his nose against the tip of Apollo's nose several times. *Beep, beep, beep.*

"Awww," I croon. "That is the cutest thing I've ever seen. But is it okay if I call him Stanley?"

"You can try, but he might not like it."

I smirk, "I'm willing to take that risk."

"Wanna hold him while I make dinner?"

"Oh! Sure."

Apollo hands him over.

I cradle him in my arms and he relaxes into me. "You don't mind if I call you Stanley, do you?" He purrs even more vigorously than he was with Apollo. "See? He likes Stanley just fine."

"He's just flirting with you."

"Does that bother you?"

"No. He knows hot pussy when he sees it."

I laugh, "You are incorrigible."

"So I've been told."

"By who? Your countless ex-girlfriends?" On several occasions when we've gone out to dinner, we've bumped into different women he used to date. All of them are model hot. It still boggles my mind he's with me.

He smiles, "No. My mom."

"Is that true?" I demand.

"Yup. She said it all the time when I was a kid. Still says it."

How does he *always* manage to say the perfect thing?

I am falling for this man so fast it scares me.

DAPHNE

"Dinner is served," Apollo says, setting two plates down on the coffee table in front of me.

"What are we eating?"

"Southwestern quinoa salad with red beans and red bell peppers, garnished with lime. The chicken is grilled, free-range, and hormone free. Avocado on the side."

"Wait, you made this while we've been talking?"

"The quinoa was cooked this morning. But yeah, I grilled the chicken fresh just now."

We start eating. "Wow, Apollo. This is incredible."

"And incredibly good for you."

"Where did you learn to cook like this?"

"The internet. Believe me, my mom didn't cook like this when I was growing up. But I just experimented with healthy stuff and figured out what I liked."

"Do you always eat like this?"

"Every night."

"Wow, will you be my own personal chef?" I joke.

"Yup. If you want." His sunshine eyes melt my heart.

I stare at him, speechless.

"What?" he chuckles.

"I—" *love you.* "Nothing. And don't talk with your mouth full. It's gross."

He snorts while chewing.

We talk about anything and everything while we eat. To my surprise, Apollo knows far more about Harry Potter than I do, and I've read all the books. Twice. He's a secret nerd and it's the cutest thing ever. Being here with him is like hanging out with my best friend after school or something. My best friend with an incredible body and a hot hard cock, that is. Not that I've ever actually seen it. But I've felt it's heat and it's girth.

He stands up and takes my empty plate.

"Do we get dessert?" I ask.

He smirks, "I'm dessert." He rinses the dishes in the sink.

Once again, I'm speechless on the couch.

When he returns, he dims the lights in the living room until it's a low glow.

He sits in the easy chair facing the couch.

Surprised, I ask, "Why are you sitting over there?"

"I believe that when a woman says no, she means no. But I'm one of those guys who never asks permission for anything. I do whatever I want. Rules and boundaries drive me up the fucking wall." He starts unbuckling his belt.

I cringe. "What are you doing?"

"What I want." He unbuttons his jeans.

"But I…"

"You can leave. You don't have to watch."

I'm glued to my seat. I'm not going anywhere. This is what I've been waiting for all my life. I think. Because this isn't how I ever imagined things would go my first time. Isn't there supposed to be a bed of rose petals in the forest? Surrounded by rainbows and unicorns? Maybe not. "Ummm, watch what?" I ask it just in case I'm totally misreading this bizarre situation.

"Watch me," he smirks and half stands up so he can push his jeans down. And his boxers. His huge cock pops out.

Hello! I want to jump right on it. But I'm afraid to move. I wish one of those unicorns was here so it could say, *It's okay, Daphne. I've got your back if anything goes wrong. I've also got a horn on my forehead if things don't work out with*—I shake my head. Stay focused. There is a loaded dick on the premises. A real dick. And it's pointing at the ceiling like a rocket launcher ready to blast off.

Apollo slumps into the easy chair and spits onto his hand before curling his slick palm around the throbbing head of his massive erection. His cock pulses every time he runs his fist down to the base.

This is easily the raunchiest and hottest thing I've ever witnessed. I can't look away.

His eyes narrow. "I've been wanting to fuck you since you walked through my front door tonight. But I'm polite." *Stroke.*

I shiver. *Don't be polite.*

"I believe a woman should be given the opportunity to make up her own mind." *Stroke. Stroke.*

Make up my mind for me because I'm stuck where I sit!

"That doesn't mean I'm not going to do something about it." *Stroke.* "I believe in clear communication." *Stroke.* "I believe in making my intentions obvious." *Stroke.* "So you know exactly where I stand." His cock is standing at full attention.

Unfortunately for me, I've lost the power of speech and have no way to communicate. Where did my words go?

"When the time is right, when we've agreed that I'm going to throw you up against the wall and fuck you until you scream, I will do exactly that. Until we have that conversation, I'm not going to make a move. Out of respect."

Let's have that conversation right now!

"Until that time, you'll just have to watch." He continues stroking himself. "I bet you're soaking wet right now."

Yep.

"I bet you want to touch yourself."

Yep.

"All you have to do is pull up that sexy dress of yours and let your fingers go to town."

Yes, I've been wearing nothing but dresses ever since he threw me up against the wall at ReaXion, hoping for a moment like this.

Too bad I'm frozen in place.

"If it was me," he chuckles, "I'd hike that dress up to your waist, tear your panties off with my teeth, and run my tongue all over that wet pussy of yours. I'd make you come so hard you'd think you'd pulled every muscle in your body."

I am dying with desire right now. I want to masturbate *so* badly. But I don't. I just squeeze my knees together like a good girl and shove my fists in my lap. It offers no relief.

"And then? When you're drenched and breathless, I'd ease my cock inside you." *Stroke.* "This cock. It would be tight at first, because you've never had a cock this big."

I've never had any cock.

"But you'd get used to it. Then you'd get addicted." *Stroke, stroke, stroke.* "You would want me to fuck you day and night for the rest of your life." *Stroke.* "Fucking…" *Stroke.* "Me and you…" *Stroke.* "Fucking like wild animals." *Stroke, stroke, stroke.*

I'm wild all right. And I've got the furry kitty to prove it. I'm sure it's rabid, based on how it's driving me crazy with lust. And it's probably frothing at the vagina, based on how wet it feels against my panties.

I squeeze my thighs together as hard as I can and whimper.

"That's what I want to hear," he mutters.

I bury my fists deep in my crotch, seeking relief.

"Go crazy, babe."

No one has ever called me babe, and it's easily the sexiest word in the English language. A shiver runs through me. No, that was an orgasm. A small one. But an orgasm nonetheless. And I'm not even really touching myself.

I have never been more turned on in my entire life.

And I'm going to do something about it.

I launch myself from the couch and stumble to the floor right between his thighs. On my knees. I rest my hands on his, mesmerized.

He pumps himself up and down. His cock is inches away from my face. If I wanted to, I could easily lick it. But I can't move because I'm hypnotized by his massive cock and just beyond it, his golden sunshine eyes, which are now burning into my soul.

"You want this, don't you, Daphne?"

Yesyesyesyesyesyesyesyes—

"You want my cock deep inside you. You want my cum deep inside you."

Uuuuuhhhhhhhh...

"You want..." his face cinches up with intense ecstasy. "This..." he strains. His cock strains too, the dark head beating with heat as it swells. His back arches, his head falls against the easy chair cushions, and he grunts.

Cum fires straight up.

Again and again.

Again.

And again.

I squeeze my thighs together and they vibrate as I desperately will myself to orgasm. But nothing happens.

Slowly, he tips his head forward, his eyes hooded but still burning bright through thin slits. He's breathing hard, slow and steady. "What do you want, Daphne?"

Cellos.

The sound of cellos.

I whisper, "I want... you."

"What do you want from me, Daphne?"

Staring into his golden eyes, I take a deep slow breath before one quivering word escapes me:

"Everything."

His sunshine smile lights up the universe, "I was hoping you'd say that."

Chapter 12

DAPHNE

We crash onto his bed.

My thighs are wrapped around his ass.

His jeans are around his ankles with his boxers.

His hard cock is jammed between my legs, thrusting against my damp panties.

We kiss hard.

Lips, tongues, teeth, biting.

It drives me wild.

He grunts, "Fucking pants." He spins to sitting and kicks his boots and socks and jeans and boxers right off. Then he spins back and yanks my panties off. His face dives between my legs.

"Oh my God!" I shout the second his tongue touches me.

He doesn't stop.

I come instantly.

He does not stop.

I fall over the edge of a mile high orgasm. It takes forever until I hit the ground.

When he comes up for air, his face shines. "Fuck you taste good."

"It's not too furry?" I giggle nervously. I don't even trim. Why would I? This has never happened before.

"I fucking love it." His face dives in again and his big arms snake up to my chest, squeezing my boobs through my dress.

I come two more times before he takes a break.

"We need to get you out of that dress." He kneels between my legs. His cock points at me like a gun. "I'm going to fuck you silly."

I laugh weakly, exhausted from all the orgasms. "I'm already silly."

"I'm just getting started."

He helps me pull my dress over my head. He's gentle compared to a moment ago. "Don't want to ruin this," he says. "I think it's my favorite dress of yours."

"It's the blue color block one I wore on our first date."

He smiles tenderly, "I remember. You're stunning in it." He sets it on his dresser, folded.

"You fold your clothes?"

"Don't you?"

"You're perfect."

"I know," he grins.

"Didn't your mom ever teach you humility?"

"No, but she taught me how to fold clothes. And treat women with respect."

"That'll work." I was so distracted by the clothes folding, I forgot that he's never seen me this naked. I cross my arms across my bra. It's the only piece of clothing I have left. I'm afraid to take it off.

"What are you doing?"

I shrug, suddenly shy.

"Take your bra off. I've been dying to see those babies since the day we met."

I'm a deer in headlights.

"Come on, Daph. I'm a boob man. Quit teasing me already. Take that bra off or I'm tearing it off."

It's now or never. I reach behind my back. I'm afraid of what he's going to say. I unhook the clasp. I shrug my shoulders. The cups fall away and...

His sunshine smile brightens the entire room. "Fuck, babe. Those are fucking perfect!" He practically tackles me on the bed and starts sucking one nipple while pinching the other.

I'm giggling the whole time.

His tongue is all over me. So are his hands. Mine are all over him, especially on his perfect washboard abs. But all of him is so damn hard. Every inch of him. All those muscles. I'm the opposite. Well, my muscles are under a layer of padding. Somehow, we're a perfect fit. Hard against soft. Opposites attract and all that.

The next thing I know, his muscled arms are planted on either side of my head and he stares down at me.

His hot hard cock lays against my wet folds.

"What are we doing, Apollo?" I whisper.

He stares at me.

"I don't have any condoms," I mutter. "Do you?"

His slow smile burns into me. He slides his hot cock slowly back and forth against my wetness.

"Do you have any condoms? I'm not on the pill."

He shakes his head, drilling me with his eyes.

"Then we can't have sex."

"Why not?" He's teasing me.

I frown. "You know why."

"Why?"

"Because of babies, dummy!"

"What if I want babies?"

"You don't want babies! We've only known each other for a few months!"

"That's long enough to know I love you, Daphne Armstrong. And that I want babies. With you."

"What! Don't be silly!"

"I'm dead serious." His words are dark and determined.

So is his stroking cock. It's driving me crazy with lust and something else that starts with L. "We can't, Apollo." I'm starting to get scared and you can hear it in my voice. "Wait. You just called me Daphne *Armstrong*, didn't you?"

His sunrise smile rises and lights up my life. "I love you, Daphne. I really do." Cellos. The sound of cellos. "You wouldn't know this, but me and you have the same easy thing my parents had. That best friend thing. I've never had that with anybody. But I do with you. It's fucking unreal. I'm more turned on right now than I've ever been with anybody. And I've been with a lot of nobodies. This isn't puppy love, Daph. This is the real deal. I want a family. I'm halfway to dead. I can't keep waiting and waiting. You know why?"

"Why?"

"Because I found you. And you're mine."

His cock pushes against my entrance.

I gasp.

He eases in slowly.

"Oh, Apollo, what are you…"

A pinch. I wince.

"Relax," he cellos. "Relax, Daph. I love you. So much. I really do."

Like that, he's in. All the way.

I am full.

"I love you too, Apollo," I whimper.

He starts a slow thrust in and out.

It feels incredible, almost too good to be true, but it's really happening. And I have no idea how he got that huge thing into me. Just snuck it right in under the radar.

"Oh my god, Apollo, this feels so good…" I moan.

"I know, babe. I know…"

He pumps slowly. Impossibly slowly.

I start to come right away. "Oh, god, Apollo. It's so… It's so… oh god! Apollo!"

His voice strains, "Cum is leaking out of my dick already, babe. I can feel it filling you up. I'm gonna come the rest of the way any second..."

"Fill me up, Apollo... Please fill me..." I'm whimpering like crazy now as the orgasm starts to build.

"Fuck," he grunts. "I can't—I can't—FUCK!!" He roars and pushes himself into me as deeply as he can, pulsing into me, his whole body vibrating as he pushes and pushes and pushes, filling me full of his cum.

"Fuck, Daphne! FUCK!!!!"

I scream out the biggest orgasm I've ever had. I scream so loud and so high I'm surprised I don't shatter his bedroom window. I'm vaguely aware that what we're doing is crazy but I'm loving every second of it.

He wants my babies.

Our babies.

<<<<<<<<>>>>>>>

DAPHNE

Two minutes later, he's pounding me from behind, one hand gripping my hip, the other furiously fingering my clit. When I feel his cum from the last time running down the inside of my thighs, it drives me wild.

I scream, "Oh god, Apollo! I can't take it! I'm going to come again!" I do. My thighs and my vagina clench hard. I know from experience that all the exercise I've been doing for the past few months makes my orgasms much stronger than I ever thought possible. It's delicious.

This time he doesn't come with me. He just keeps fucking me.

A few minutes later, I come again, harder than before. It's so powerful I can't even keep myself up on all fours so I collapse to the mattress. He falls with me, on top, and just keeps fucking. I open my legs and arch my back so my ass is in the air and he has complete access. The head of his cock rubs across a sweet spot deep inside me that I didn't know I had. My body starts to buzz.

It's like my orgasm never stopped.

I just keep coming and coming.

He thrusts and thrusts, swelling larger than before, groaning and grunting like an insane caveman.

He grabs my hair and pulls hard. He breathes heat into my ear and growls, "You are the hottest fucking woman on this planet. And you are mine, babe. All. Fucking. Mine. I'm gonna fuck you so hard you forget your own name. And I'm gonna fill you up with so much cum, the only thing you'll be able to remember is *my* name. Mine. Say my name, Daphne. Say it."

"I'm yours, Apollo. All yours."

"Forever mine."

"Forever yours."

"Forever," he hisses. He starts to grunt like maybe he's dying but when he starts to pulse, I know he's coming alive inside me.

I go right back over the edge of a sky-high orgasm and I scream.

DAPHNE

"I've been wanting to do this for months," I purr.

He lies on his back with his hands clasped behind his head. "Me too."

I swing my knee over his waist like I'm getting on a horse. Which I sort of am. Because he has horse cock. I plant my heels on the bed and rest one palm on his muscled chest while I reach between my legs and position him. I'm so wet, he slides right in. But I take it slow. My legs are strong enough now that it's easy.

I can't imagine doing him like this a few months ago. I would've been out of breath in three seconds.

I lift myself up then ease slowly back down. I get into a rhythm, focusing all my attention on pleasuring him.

The whole time I'm doing it, his entire body is tense and he shakes all over. Even his toes shake. He unclasps his hands from behind his head and holds them up near his face, shaking them too. It's almost like he's being electrocuted, it's so intense. "Fuck, Daphne! Fuck! Your pussy is a velvet vice! God damn it!!"

"All those squats," I smirk, loving that I'm driving him wild.

After a good ten minutes of this, I'm surprised I haven't killed him with pleasure. I slowly sit down and change up my squatting motion to a grind.

"Don't stop," he begs in a hoarse whisper.

I start to arc my pelvis against him. When my clit slides across his skin, every cell in my body lights up and starts to dance. This motion hits my clit just right. Now we're both being electrocuted with pleasure.

"Fuck, Daph. Like that. Just. Like. That." He drops his head into the pillows and groans.

We literally fuck for another three hours.

Every single time he comes, he shoots his cum inside me.

Every single time is better than the last.

I'm pretty sure I started ovulating yesterday.

After this, there's no way I'm not pregnant.

DAPHNE

It's nearly 4:00 a.m.

I lie curled against Apollo starting to doze off.

Both of us are on top of the covers, totally naked, totally drenched, totally spent.

He whispers, "I'd ask you to marry me, but I don't want to scare you off. So I'll wait until after you meet my mom. She has to approve."

My eyes pop open and I tense.

"Joking. She'll love you. And I don't ask her approval for anything. Ask her. She'll tell you," he chuckles. "I never listen. Anyway, you wanna marry me?"

I bite my lip. "Am I dreaming all this? I mean, seriously. Ouch! Did you just flick my arm again?!"

"Yeah."

"I hate you!"

"I hate you too. In fact, I will hate you with all my heart until the day I die. I hope you're okay with that."

I pinch the sensitive skin on his ribs.

"Hey! What the fuck was that?!"

"I'm not marrying anyone who hates me."

Silence.

"Was that a yes?" he mutters.

"No, it was a no. Hater." I giggle and pinch him again.

"Ow! Okay, okay! If I promise to love you with all my heart until my dying day, will you marry me?" Cellos.

I bite my lower lip. "I—"

"Meow!" Stanley jumps up on the bed, purring.

Apollo chuckles, "Say hello to your new mama, Stink Foot."

"Can we agree to call him Stanley?"

"Can we agree you'll marry me?"

"Yes."

"Stanley it is." He pulls me against him and we kiss.

Stanley purrs.

I want to cry. Happy tears.

After a moment, he says thoughtfully, "I have to warn you of one thing."

"Should I be worried?" I giggle.

"Only if you hate coming on my cock."

"That's what you're warning me about?"

"No. From now on, I'm going to take you whenever I feel like it. Can we agree on that?"

My eyes widen. "Ummmm… Define whenever."

"Whenever is whenever. It's a simple question. Yes or no?"

"Yes."

He chuckles with sinful mischief. "Be careful what you wish for…"

Chapter 13

DAPHNE

"You know what I love about you?" he asks in the morning as we stand in his small bathroom in front of the mirror. By morning, I mean noon because we just woke up.

"What's that?" Right now, my hair is a giant fuzz bomb and it looks terrible.

"Your hair. It looks like a sexplosion."

"A what?"

"You heard me."

"*You're* the sexplosion." I eye his perfect body in the mirror. It inspires lust, as always.

"No, I'm serious. I love it. It's so… what's the opposite of virile? I mean, what's the woman's version?"

"You read all those books. Don't you know?"

"Harry Potter doesn't go into details about sex stuff. Oh! I remember. Fertile. Your hair looks so damn fertile."

"Are you trying to get me pregnant our first time?"

He smirks, "No. But I'm praying to the gods that you do. I don't want you going anywhere."

Cellos. Every time he speaks, it's cellos and my heart melts.

"By the way, that was your first time, wasn't it?" he asks.

"Yeah. Is that okay?"

"For me it was perfect. I just hope you don't mind only ever sleeping with one guy."

I turn around and wrap my arms around him. My full breasts brush against the dusting of hair on his muscled abs. I hood my eyes and look up at him. I grin the sexiest grin I can. "I think I'll manage."

"I love you, Mrs. Armstrong. With all my heart. You're the woman I've always wanted. Always." He kisses the top of my fuzz bomb gently and chuckles, "I know there's a head in there somewhere…"

I sigh sweetly. "I love you too."

"Meow!" Stanley's tail brushes around my calves.

I giggle, "And you too, Stanley."

"Meow!"

I glare up at Apollo.

He frowns, "What?"

"How could you ever call him Stink Foot? He's probably traumatized."

He laughs, "Are you kidding? He's totally my bitch."

"Am I your bitch?" I ask coquettishly.

"Hell no you're not."

"I'm not?" I growl.

"And you're nobody else's bitch either. I catch anyone saying that and I swear to Christ I'll…" he exhales.

I narrow my eyes. "You'll what? Defend me? Protect my honor? Slay my enemies?"

"I thought you didn't like violence?"

"I don't. But a girl likes to know that a man has her back."

His smile turns into a smirk. "Okay then I'll sic Stink Foot on them!" He dashes out of the bathroom. "Dude is wicked with his claws!"

I chase him into the bedroom and the next thing I know we're twisted in the rumpled sheets and he's deep inside me.

My heart and my body.

It's the only place I ever want him to be.

DAPHNE

"Is it okay that I'm nervous?" I ask as we walk toward the sidewalk cafe on Sunset Boulevard near Apollo's Hollywood apartment. The sun is bright and warm, just like Apollo.

"A better question," he chuckles, "is if it's okay that we're so damn late. It's almost one. A little late for brunch. I hope she's not pissed."

I'm really nervous. "Ummm…"

"There she is!" He waves and I follow his gaze.

I don't know what I was expecting with Apollo's mom. No, I do. I was expecting a dainty super model like Fashion Forty Fiona. But his mom looks like… him. She's easily six feet tall and she's gorgeous. She wears a hint of mascara and her golden eyes shine just like Apollo's. Like me, she's stocky. You can't miss it despite the camouflage of her patterned maxi dress. She hides her figure like I do. She even has big hair. Not frizzy and nearly coal black like mine, but wavy and dark brown.

That's when it all makes sense.

This isn't a fantasy. My bubble is not going to burst. It's not some fluke that Apollo is attracted to me. I look like a darker haired and shorter version of his mom. It makes perfect sense that he's attracted to me.

Oh, wait.

He doesn't have a mommy thing, does he?

You know what?

Who cares if he does?

There has to be something about him that isn't perfect because everything else is. Now the only thing I have to worry about is whether or not his mom likes me. And how short the apron strings are.

"You must be Daphne," she pulls me into a hug. She hugs big. Just like Apollo. "Apollo has told me so much about you."

I hope she's not domineering. Domineering is good when it comes to a hot hunky husband, but not when it comes to your husband's mother. I hope he didn't take after her...

Apollo chuckles, "Mom, I haven't told you anything about her."

"I know her name," she scoffs. "And I know she's one of your work clients. That's something."

Apollo smiles at me, "I figured Mom could get to know you in person. I can't really do you justice."

That doesn't sound like a mama's boy to me. I laugh, "Ummm..."

"Ignore him. I'm Michelle. Pleased to meet you."

We shake hands.

I'm starting to like her.

Apollo says, "You two get to know each other while I put our name on the list."

"I already did," Michelle says.

"Okay. Then I'll go use the restroom while you two get to know each other." He tears open the front door of the crowded cafe and strides inside.

Michelle shakes her head, "Aren't you sick of him yet? He's such a pain in the rear."

"I don't mind," I giggle. I'm shaking with nerves as I try to figure out Michelle. I'm not sure if she's being polite or if this is a front.

"I'm kidding. Apollo is a good kid. I mean man. I swear, he was sixteen just yesterday. You would've hated him back then. A complete scoundrel."

I wince, "Do I want to hear this?" Now I'm really uncomfortable.

She stares at me for a second, the smile on her face quivering. She takes a deep breath and shakes her head. "I'm sorry, Daphne. I can see you're nervous. I'm nervous too." She completely means it.

I suddenly feel much better. "Why?"

She glances into the cafe briefly, like she's checking for Apollo to make sure he's not about to walk back outside and interrupt our moment. She whispers, "He told me you were *the one* and I had to meet you. He's never told me any woman was *the one*. This is a big deal. For you *and* me. I really want to like you, sweetheart."

I laugh, nervous again. "Ummm... me too."

"Oh, I'm ruining this, Daphne. I'm really sorry. He's my only son. He's..." Her eyes shimmer. "He's all I have left of James. His father." She bites her lower lip, fighting back tears, "I miss that man so much. I miss him every day." Her body shakes. "I'm sorry, I promised myself I wouldn't cry when I met you." She uses her pinky to scrape away a tear from the corner of her eye. She sniffs, "I just want my son to be happy. Promise me you'll make him happy?"

I feel my heart open wide to this woman because I can feel hers wide open to me. Now I want to cry too. "I will. Promise." I laugh and my eyes are watering.

"What did you do to her?" Apollo demands with a chuckle, suddenly back outside with us on the sunshine sidewalk.

Michelle sniffles, "Who, me? Or her?"

"The both of you. What's with the crying party out here? Did somebody die?"

"Shut up," Michelle laughs and nudges Apollo's arm with her elbow. "I'm embarrassed enough as it is."

"What do you have to be embarrassed about, Mom?"

She frowns, "I want your girlfriend to like me, that's what!"

"I do," I giggle. I really do.

A waiter sticks his head out the front door and calls out, "Armstrong, party of three!!"

Apollo wraps his arm around me and smiles his sunshine smile. "That's us. The Armstrong family. All three of us."

I melt into his side.

And like that, I know we'll be best friends forever.

I can't explain it.

I just do.

Apollo Armstrong is my forever man.

Really and truly.

Chapter 14

DAPHNE

Six months later.

"You can do it, Lynn! One more rep!" I cheer.

She glares at me, sweat dripping down her face. "When I signed up for this, I did it so I could get squat fucked, not ass fucked."

We both laugh as she strains to lift the empty bar to standing.

She walks it to the rack and sets it down. "How did you ever talk me into this?"

"It was your idea, remember?"

"You're a liar, you know that?"

I laugh.

It's true. I talked her into it. But it took a lot of talking.

Ever since I quit my job as a dental receptionist two months ago, I've been working here at Body Fitness as a personal trainer. It wasn't hard to get the job because I'm sleeping with the new head trainer. Yes, Apollo got promoted. It also helps that he and I talk about healthy eating and healthy living every single day. Maybe it's obsessive, but at least we're obsessing about staying healthy. And we're doing it together. There's worse things to base a relationship on.

Anyway, deciding to work here was the logical next step for me because I was already spending all my free time here exercising or hanging out with Apollo whenever he wasn't with a client. So why not work here? When I told Lynn I got the job, she said she'd be my first client. When I told her I had signed her up for a trial membership, it took a bit of convincing to get her to come in. But eventually she agreed. I've been training her ever since.

She blots her forehead with her workout towel. "I miss you at lunch, girl."

"I miss you too."

She smiles and pats my arm. "This is the right place for you."

I nod. "It is."

"You're so lucky you get to work with your man."

"You could work with Matt. He has an office staff. Can't you be a receptionist for him?"

"Are you kidding?" she laughs. "We'd kill each other. Trust me. When you've been married eleven years, you'll know what I mean."

I smile. "You're probably right."

She grins, "I hope I'm wrong. I'm no prize. Then again, neither is Matt. But I love the man. What can I say? True love is blind dumb."

I snort, "Ummm, how is that romantic again?"

"Love isn't romance. Love is work. Take my kids for example."

"Dylan and Nicholas? What about them?"

"No, take them!" She pleads. "Just for the weekend! So I can have some peace and quiet for once!" She laughs heartily. "I'm kidding. I love those two little firecrackers. But I'm telling you, true love is work. Relationships aren't fairy tales."

"I know." I really don't. But I'll take her word for it.

Apollo waves and saunters over. "She busting your ladyballs again, Lynn?"

"All busted," she chuckles.

"Good to see you here again, Lynn. Daphne tells me you've been coming along great with the training program."

"Working on it. But I'm all trained out for the night. Now I need to hit the showers. I also need to have you two over to the house for dinner. I think my husband Matt could learn a thing or two from you about squat spotting." She winks at Apollo.

Apollo narrows his eyes. "What?"

Lynn nods at me, "Ask her."

I blush like roses.

"Bye you two!" Lynn catches my eye. "See you Thursday?"

"Yeah. For sure. Same time?"

"Eight o'clock. It's the earliest I can get here after I cook the kids dinner. And by kids, I include Matt." She waves as she wanders to the locker room.

Apollo arches an eyebrow. "What... did you tell her... about squatting?"

"Ummm," I chuckle. "That was a long time ago. When we first met."

"Did you tell her what we did that day? The *mmmm* and the *mmmm*?"

I wince, "I hope that's okay."

"No. It's not okay." The light goes out of his eyes.

"It's not?"

"No. That was our thing. Now you're telling everybody?"

"It's just Lynn! She won't tell anybody! She hasn't even told her husband Matt!"

"Doesn't matter," he glowers. "I'll still have to teach you a lesson for being such a naughty little girl." Then he winks and the sunshine is back in his eyes, but it's dark, like an eclipse. "I just have to figure out what form of punishment will give you the most excruciating... *orgasm*."

"Oh! That sounds like my kind of punishment. Do tell."

"No, I won't tell. I'll make you pay for your mistake when you least expect it."

"Mmmmm. Deal. But I still have another client tonight."

"Better watch your back then," he warns with a wink.

"What did you have in mind?" I smile.

He grins, "Actually, I'll be in the lap pool while you're with your client. Need to blow off some steam."

"I can do some blowing for you," I giggle.

"Maybe later. But you can't enjoy it. It has to be punishment."

"How do you expect me *not* to enjoy sucking your cock?" I mean it. It's one of my favorite pastimes. And his.

"Good point," he chuckles. "We'll hammer out the details of your punishment after I finish swimming."

"You can do all the *hammering* you want..."

"I get it," he smiles. "You want sex tonight. Let me finish my laps so we can go home and do it right."

"Okay. If you insist. But do I get to see you in your sexy Speedo before you dive in?"

"Maybe after," he smiles and walks to the men's locker room.

My new client is a friend of Lynn's. I've never met her before tonight. Her name is Anne and she reminds me of me, except younger. We have so much fun chatting together during her session that we lose track of time and finish up late. By the time she leaves, it's nearly closing time and the gym is empty.

I make my way to the locker room to shower and change. I never would've imagined when I first came into Body Fitness that I would feel confident enough to shower here, but I do. It's not a nightly routine, but I often do it when Apollo and I have dinner plans like tonight. We're going to ReaXion to celebrate our one year anniversary.

I grab my shower tote from my locker and make my way to one of the shower stalls and pull the curtain closed. As always, I'm wearing my flip-flops. I don't care how clean they keep the showers. Some precautions are worth the dorkishness. I put my hair up in a bun because we don't have an hour for me to deal with it after it gets wet. Then I turn on the water and rinse myself under the warm spray.

The second I close my eyes, I think of Apollo. He's all I think about these days. Somehow, that feels just right. I never thought I'd be so content in life, but I am. Because of him. And I'm—

SHRIK!!

The shower curtain whips open behind me and I instantly feel cold air on my back. I spin around and wipe water out of my eyes.

Apollo stands there nearly naked, wearing the smallest navy blue swimsuit known to man. His cock is rock hard and poking out above the waistband. This poking cock look is either dead sexy or the cheesiest thing I've ever seen. I take a second look. Nope, dead sexy.

He's also wearing flip flops.

That is the cheesiest thing I've ever seen. But I don't even care. I laugh, "What are you doing in here? This is the women's locker room!"

"We're closed. There's nobody here." He pulls the shower curtain shut behind him.

"So?! It's the principle! You're invading my personal space!"

"I'm gonna be invading a lot more than your personal space in a second. And the only principle you need to worry about is the principle I'm gonna put up inside you while you're screaming my name. I can't believe you're not pregnant yet."

A small voice in the corner of my heart whispers: *One of you is sterile. Or both of you.* I ignore it. After six months of unprotected sex with the love of my life, I've gotten very good at ignoring that voice. "Then you better do something about that and start your invasion, Mr. Man."

He grabs my wet butt with both hands and yanks me hard against him. His mouth smashes into mine and we kiss deeply. I roll his Speedo down and his cock pops out hard and strong between us.

I must be barren.

I push the thought away because I'm soaking wet. And I'm not talking about the water raining down on my shoulders from the shower. I'm talking about the wetness raining between my legs.

He's sterile.

I don't want to think about it.

He hoists me up and I wrap my strong thighs around his waist.

He positions his throbbing head against my opening and I ease down.

He hisses, "Fuck, Daph. Every time I'm inside you it feels like the first fucking time I've ever had sex with anybody."

"I know, love. I know."

Apollo is so strong, he easily holds me up while fucking me. I help, using my legs. I never imagined I would have this much stamina or be this strong. A year ago, I couldn't climb a flight of stairs without losing my breath.

Since then, Apollo and I have gotten *really* good at sex. We frequently have hour long sex sessions. I'm talking multiple times per week. Some weekends, we go even longer. But some times, we do it quick like this. We're in a gym shower after all, not our apartment. Yes, I moved in with Apollo a month ago. It seemed like the right time.

As he lifts me up his cock, I clench my pussy around him before lowering myself back down. As always, our sex is magic and beyond anything I ever expected sex could be.

I whisper, "I love this fucking cock of yours."

He murmurs in my ear, "Dirty talking now, are we?"

"Uh huh."

"That's a first," he chuckles, continuing his slow thrusts, filling me perfectly. "I could do this all night."

"If it was our shower I could. But I want dinner," I whine as I climb up his cock.

"Worked up an appetite?" He thrusts.

"Uh huh." I ease back down his cock.

"I've been watching you all day. Thinking about fucking you in this shower." *Thrust.*

"Then fuck me, you stud." *Slide.*

"You better believe I'm gonna fuck you. I'm gonna make you scream my name so loud they hear you in the movie theaters next door."

I giggle at that.

"I can hear the two of you just fine!" Fashion Forty Fiona grumbles on the other side of the shower curtain. "Would you two hurry the fuck up and fuck so I can go home?"

I stifle a laugh by biting Apollo's muscled shoulder.

He grunts, "Get the fuck out of here, Fiona!"

"This is the women's locker room, Apollo!" she says snidely.

"I'm fucking my wife, Fiona! Take a fucking hike!"

"Your wife?" she blurts.

He growls, "Yes, my wife! Now leave already!"

"Just hurry the fuck up so I can go home," she groans and walks off. Although Apollo is the head trainer, Fiona is responsible for locking up at closing.

"Fuck her," Apollo mutters. "I'm not hurrying anything. She can fucking wait." He resumes thrusting into me and I match his timing, grinding down against him.

"Did you call me your wife?" We've never made it official. No engagement, no ceremony. We just live together.

"Yeah I did. I told you almost a year ago I was going to marry you."

"I thought that was a figure of speech."

"It wasn't. You're gonna have my kids."

Sterile.

I suddenly get all emotional. "I would love that." I'm going to cry.

His eyes glimmer and his voice goes hoarse. "I mean it, Daph. You're going to have my babies. Okay?" He suddenly sounds so uncertain.

Barren.

He's thinking the same thing.

"Yeah," I nod, "Okay."

"You mean it?" He sounds emotional, like maybe he's on the verge of tears.

"I mean it," I nod vigorously.

It's not like we've never discussed the fact that I still haven't gotten pregnant. We've discussed seeing fertility specialists. We've even discussed adoption in a round about way. Mainly, we avoid the topic because I think it hurts us both too much.

"Oh my god, Apollo, I'm coming..." I'm also weeping as the orgasm starts to shake me. Every muscle in my body clamps down.

"I love you, Daphne. I love you so fucking much." His face tightens with emotion.

"I love you too, babe. I love you—oh my god!!!" My face knots and I bite his shoulder and I come even harder and he fires his seed into me.

He sucks in a sob and fires again and again.

A wave pulses up my core, milking him, trying to draw out every last drop. I sink down, taking in every inch of him.

In that moment, our hearts connect.

In that moment, something deep and profound opens between us.

Something eternal.

Chapter 15

DAPHNE

"Do you want dessert?" Apollo asks two hours later at ReaXion. We sit side by side in one of the back booths. Our usual booth. We learned after my first time here to call ahead for reservations.

"Dessert? Who stole my boyfriend?" I lift up his top lip and peer into his mouth. "Is there a robot cyborg in there?"

He snickers. "We can have dessert once in a while. Besides, we're celebrating."

"Celebrating what?"

"Hello! Our one year anniversary. I thought the guy was the one who was supposed to forget, not the girl."

I giggle, "I didn't forget. I actually got you something." I reach into my purse and pull out a card.

"What's this?"

"Open it."

He peels the envelope open and slides out the card. There's a picture of a cartoon donkey on the front. He reads it out loud. "To the biggest ass I know?" He glares at me. "What the hell kind of card is this?"

"Read it," I giggle.

He opens the card. "Happy Burrothday? That's fucking stupid," he chuckles. "It's not even my birthday."

"I thought you'd like it anyway."

He kisses my cheek. "I love it."

"Open the other envelope."

Inside the card is a small white envelope. "Money, I hope." He winks at me and opens it. His eyes go big. "Two tickets to Universal Studios Florida!"

"You know what that means," I grin.

"The Wizarding World of Harry Potter! That's what that shit means! And you know what else?"

"What?"

"Butterbeer! I've been wanting to try that stuff ever since I read about it in the books!"

"Me too," I giggle.

He stares at the tickets for a long time and his brows slowly knit.

"This is too much, Daph. It's gonna cost an arm and a leg to fly down there and stay at the hotel."

I shrug shyly. "I've been saving up for a special occasion."

"For how long?"

"Pretty much since forever."

"It's not like we're rich. Are you sure we can afford this?"

I love that he keeps calling us a we. "Sure. Don't worry about it."

"Are you sure?"

"Yes already! We're going to go see Harry Potter. And drink butterbeer."

He kisses me on the lips. "I love you, babe. I got you something too."

"What?"

"Dessert."

"Oh." I'm a little disappointed.

He waves at our waiter, who nods back before walking into the kitchen. A moment later he pushes out a dessert cart loaded with every decadent dessert imaginable. "What would the lady like?"

"Ummm, we're not eating everything, are we?"

"No," Apollo chuckles. "But we can taste everything. I figure one bite of each adds up to one full dessert. Unless you've been sneaking desserts when I'm not looking?"

"No!" It's true. I rarely eat desserts anymore. It's not hard to skip them when Apollo is my dessert every night.

"I know you've been a good girl. So tonight, we can enjoy ourselves."

The whole time we've been talking, the waiter has been setting plate after plate on our table.

"This is ridiculous," I laugh. "I'm surrounded by chocolate and frosting and every flavor of cake imaginable."

Apollo wraps an arm around me. "Everyone deserves to be ridiculous once in a while. One other thing." He pulls an envelope out of his back pocket.

It's bent from him sitting on it. I open it immediately. It's a fancy white card like you find at those boutique stationary stores. The front is embossed and has gold script printed in the middle that reads: *Your reservation...* I open it and scan the inside, reading aloud. "Hotel Del Coronado. One ocean view suite for two, Saturday, March—that's tomorrow! Are you taking me on a weekend getaway? For our anniversary?"

"Yup. To San Diego."

I throw my arms around him and kiss him all over his face. It's the first official trip we've been on. We don't exactly have a lot of money.

He nods at the waiter.

The waiter pulls a small gift bag out from under the dessert cart and hands it to me. "You two enjoy yourselves," he says before walking away with the empty cart.

"Is there more?" I gasp.

"Open it," Apollo grins.

I reach into the gift bag and pull out an electric blue... bikini. "You did not," I chuckle.

"Did too." Apollo's eyes are all sunshine. "You know I've always loved you in blue. It makes your blue diamonds shine." He gazes right into my eyes. His are liquid gold.

"Apollo..." I moan, my eyes wet.

He grins, "Since we'll be at the beach tomorrow, I can finally see you frolic in the San Diego waves in a bikini like I've always dreamed."

"As long as I get to see you in your teensy-weensy Speedo."

"Deal. But we both know my weensy is not teensy."

We both cackle with laughter.

Never in my life would I have thought I'd be wearing a bikini. In public, no less. Will I look like a Sports Illustrated swimsuit model?

No.

But you damn well better bet I'll be wearing it!

Unless...

I stare at the table full of desserts in front of us. "Are we going to eat all this? I don't think I'll be able to fit into this bikini tomorrow if we do."

"Like I said, just take one bite of everything. And, if it'll help, I'll stick my hand up your dress and finger you the whole time. You'll be too busy coming on my fingers to eat."

My eyes flare, "Deal!"

DAPHNE

"I hope it's not too late for breakfast," I giggle as we stumble out of our room at the Hotel Del Coronado on Sunday morning. "I wanted to have French Toast."

"You should've thought of that before you climbed into the shower with me."

"Don't blame me! I just wanted to give you a blow job but you insisted on a four course meal."

He chuckles, "What can I say? I never get tired of eating your pussy." He says it *right* as we're passing a silver haired woman in the hallway.

"Disgusting!" She gasps, her eyes bugging out.

Apollo leans against me and whispers, "She's only acting like that because she can't remember what it's like to have anyone go down on her."

I giggle, "You won't let me forget, will you?"

"Hell no."

We walk downstairs and outside to the Sheerwater Restaurant overlooking the ocean. We're seated at a table near the green lawn.

I ask the waiter, "Is it too late for breakfast?"

"Not at all, madam."

Apollo and I order French Toast, no powdered sugar of course. But I do pour the thinnest drizzle of maple syrup on mine. Since I eat so little sugar these days it's more than enough.

We eat.

"Wow, that was incredible," I moan after finishing mine.

Apollo finished his ten minutes ago. He eats like a vacuum cleaner. "You want some dessert?"

"We had dessert last night."

"Yeah, but you only tried half of everything."

I glare, "That's because you had your hand up my dress!"

"You agreed. So don't blame me."

I smile, "I love you, you sex maniac."

"Me too. So, dessert?"

"Do they even have dessert for breakfast?"

"I told you I never follow the rules."

"Okay. Fine. What are we having this time?"

"Have you ever had blue velvet cake?"

"I thought it was red velvet cake."

"I had them make it special."

When he catches our waiter's eye, the man nods and strides toward the kitchen, much like the waiter did at ReaXion on Friday night.

"You sure planned out this weekend," I chuckle.

He grins, "Yup."

A minute later, the waiter carries out a silver tray that holds a single wedge of blue velvet cake with white buttercream frosting. A lone candle pokes from the top, already lit.

The waiter stops at the table. "Would the lady like her cake?"

I clap my hands over my mouth. "Oh my God, is that a..."

Apollo smiles and nods at the waiter, who sets the tray on the table before walking off.

A ring with two blue diamonds circles the base of the candle.

"Oh my god, Apollo. What did you do?" I'm crying now.

"I'm marrying you, Daph. What does it look like?"

"Oh, Apollo. This is too much."

He lifts the plate with the cake off the silver tray and holds it in front of me.

The candle burns. The blue diamonds are beautiful and catch the sunlight magnificently.

He says, "Daphne Bowman, will you do me the honor of becoming Mrs. Armstrong?"

"Yes!"

"And will you do me the honor of being my wife and my forever love?"

"Yes!"

"And will you bear our children and be the best mother our kids can possibly have?"

"Yuh-yes." I say it because I *want* it to be true. I want to be a mother. I want to raise *our* children. Even if it isn't meant to be, I still want it. I almost say out loud, *I don't care if we never have children, Apollo. As long as I have you, as long as we have each other, that's all that matters.* But I don't because I don't want to ruin this moment. "Yes, of course." I sniffle and reach out to hug him.

"Hold up. Make a wish and blow the candle out first. So I can put the ring on your finger."

I bite my lower lip, "Ummm... I wish for..." I break into soft laughter. The tears are coming.

"Don't tell me. It's your wish. It has to be secret or else it won't come true." His eyes shimmer.

"Okay, okay." I'm crying. Good thing I'm not wearing any makeup this morning. I look him straight in the eyes. "I love you, Apollo. I love you so much."

I close my eyes and hope with all my heart.

I wish for...

Epilogue

One year later.

Wishes do come true.

"I put them down for the night," I whisper as I sink into the leather couch next to Apollo.

"Are they sleeping?" he whispers.

"Like babies," I grin.

You would think I'd have gotten pregnant that first time Apollo and I had sex. We had so much sex that night *and* I was ovulating. We also had sex every day and night thereafter. You would also think I would've gotten pregnant the fiftieth time or the hundredth time. But I didn't. It took nine more wonderful months of trying. We must have had sex almost 1,000 times before his seed finally took hold.

But it did.

I think it happened either that time in the shower at Body Fitness or at the Hotel Del after he proposed. We'll never know for sure.

But his seed took root in my womb.

Twice.

We have twins.

Roman and Rema.

Yes, they're sort of named after the twin brothers Romulus and Remus who founded Rome. It was Apollo's idea. Since Rema is a girl, I insisted we change the names up a bit. He agreed.

Soon we'll have to move into a bigger place. The twins have almost outgrown their bassinets. I don't think we can fit two cribs in our lone bedroom unless we remove our bed. We'll probably end up putting the cribs in the living room until we move.

I was a little worried about how Stanley Stink Foot would respond to the arrival of Roman and Rema. But the moment we came home from the hospital, he was sniffing around the babies like a proud new daddy cat. He loves the kids like they're his own kittens. Every night he sleeps at the foot of their bassinets, standing guard.

I adjust the waistband of my yoga pants. "I can't believe how much weight I gained during the pregnancy. I'm still fat."

"You look great," he smiles.

"You are such a liar." I don't care. I love that he always knows what to say to make me feel better. "It's going to take forever to lose it."

"What are you talking about? You weigh less now than when I met you."

I gasp, "You're right!" I will never be thin by mainstream standards, but I will be strong and healthy for the rest of my life.

"See? You're already ahead of the game."

I smirk, "I don't know if I'd go that far. These yoga pants feel like a sausage casing and I'm the sausage."

"You're my sausage." He grins his sunshine grin, pulling me into his arms. "Don't worry. We'll fuck the baby weight right off you."

I smile, "Can we start fucking now?"

"After the movie."

"Okay," I groan.

"Can I start it?"

"Go for it."

He leans forward and hits the spacebar on his laptop. "I still can't believe you've never seen this."

I roll my eyes. "What do you expect? My life has been a whirlwind for the past year. Anyway, what is it about again?"

"It's about Rocky Balboa. The bossest badass ever to enter the ring."

"It's not violent, is it?" I ask.

"I'll tell you when to close your eyes. The part when Rocky cuts a guy's head off with a chainsaw is pretty gruesome."

"Chainsaws!!! I thought you said this was a boxing movie!"

"I'm kidding. No chainsaws."

"And let me guess, no love story either. Right?"

He smiles, "Actually, it has a great love story. In fact, it's almost as good as ours." He winks. "Almost. But not quite."

I swoon. "I love you, Apollo."

He winks, "But you'll hate Apollo Creed."

When the movie finishes, I am jumping out of my seat. "Why didn't you show me this movie a year ago?! This is the best movie I've ever seen!!"

Apollo frowns, "Are you kidding? There was blood everywhere by the fifteenth round! Both fighters nearly died in the ring! I thought you said you didn't like violence!"

"I still don't! But Rocky and Adrian ended up together! And now I'm all inspired to exercise! Where's a staircase? I want to run through the streets of Philadelphia before running up a hundred flights of stairs followed by a thousand cheering kids screaming my name! Daph-ne! Daph-ne! Daph-ne! I'll jog my baby weight off in no time!!"

He grins his rugged sunshine grin, "You know what they say: fitness is a lifestyle."

I jump up from the couch. "I want the Rocky theme to be my lifestyle theme song! I feel like I can do anything right now!" I start singing the theme song in a low voice so I don't wake the babies. "Getting strong now!!"

Apollo chuckles, "Rocky is a great movie, isn't it?"

"Yeah it is!" I dance around the living room, whispering the theme song over and over. When I run out of breath, I plop back down next to him on the couch.

He pulls me into his arms and kisses me on the cheek. "I told you you would love every minute of it."

I get all weepy and look him in the eyes. "And I'll love every minute of the rest of our lives together."

"Damn right you will. I will too. Because I've got the hottest wife on the planet."

"Do not," I giggle.

He jams his fingers between my legs. "Do too."

I squeeze my thighs together, trapping his hand. "You know, the doctor said we could have sex six weeks ago."

He kisses me gently. "Yeah, but I wanted to make sure you were completely healed."

"I was completely healed six weeks ago."

"Maybe if I had a small dick. But I'm gonna bore you out, woman."

I chuckle, "The babies already bored me out. I'm like a wind tunnel down there."

"Oh yeah?"

The next thing I know, I feel his fingers worm down the front of my yoga pants and under the waistband of my panties.

"Mmmm," he grins. "You're wet."

I smirk, "It's all those sexy boxers fighting in the ring. Not you."

"You wish."

His fingers find my clit.

"Oh…" I moan. Then they press inside me. "Mmmm. Keep doing that."

"Feels like a velvet vice to me."

"Then you better do something about it. It'll be feeding time for Roman and Rema sooner than you think. We've got maybe an hour."

"Then for the next hour, it's my feeding time…" He yanks my yoga pants down along with my panties and dives face first between my legs.

I'm writhing and moaning a second later. When I come hard, I do my best not to scream so I don't wake the twins.

He lifts his slick face up and his sunshine grin lights up my world. "I will never get tired of eating this beautiful furry pussy of yours." He pushes his sweats down and kicks them off before pulling his T-shirt over his head. As always, his body is rock hard. So is his cock. "And I will never get tired of fucking this beautiful body of yours." He lowers himself between my legs and slides right in, filling me to the hilt. As he starts thrusting, he stares into my eyes and mutters, "Daphne, you are the most beautiful woman I have ever known, inside and out. And every inch of you is mine to take."

I grab his ass and pull him into me. "Every inch of *you* is mine to take, Mr. Horse Cock."

Thanks to Apollo, and a whole lot of hard work on my part, I took my beauty back.

And I will hold onto it forever.

Just like I'll hold onto Apollo.

And our children.

If it hadn't been for those cellos, none of this ever would've happened.

<<<<<<<<>>>>>>>

APOLLO

Five years later.

"Hey, Dad. I've got some people I want you to meet." I squat down in the grass beside his San Diego hillside tombstone. "Say hello to your grandkids."

"Roman! Rema!" Daphne calls out. "Come over here! Your daddy wants to show you something!"

The twins are chasing each other around on the lush lawn. They run over to their mother, laughing.

"You're it!"

"No, you're it!"

"Okay, you two," Daphne grins, "Settle down for a moment."

I cross my legs beside Dad's grave.

Roman and Rema tumble into my lap, giggling. They both immediately attack me.

I chuckle, "Wrestling later! Daddy wants to tell you something."

"What?!"

"Tell us!"

Daphne and I never really talked about when we would tell the kids about my father, their grandfather. But they started asking the last time we visited my mom's house and saw all the pictures of Dad she still keeps out. So we made this trip today special for them.

I say. "Roman, Rema, do you see this grave?"

Rema leans forward and runs her finger over the raised brass letters. She gasps. "That says Michelle Armstrong! Is that Grandma Michelle?!" She's terrified. "Did she die?"

"Noooo," Daphne croons. "You just saw Grandma Michelle last week. She's fine."

"Then who is James?" Rema asks.

I hug both of my children against my chest. My voice is tight. "Grandpa James was my daddy."

"Is he died?" Roman asks.

I kiss the top of his head.

Daphne is kneeling behind me, rubbing my back.

"Yes, sweetie," I say to Roman. "Grandpa James passed away before you were born. Before I met your mother, in fact."

"Oh." Roman says solemnly.

"Why did he die?" Rema asks.

"Because his heart was sick," I say softly.

"Oh," Rema says.

I kiss the top of her head. "I want you two to know that your Grandpa James loves you very much."

"But he's dead," Rema says. "How can he love us?"

"Because love lasts forever. And I know that he loves you almost as much as I love you."

"He doesn't love us the same?" Rema asks.

I smile and squeeze her. "No. No one loves you as much as I do. I mean, no one except your Mommy."

Rema smiles at Daphne, "Mommy, I love you the same as Daddy."

Daphne says, "I know you do, sweetie. I know."

"I do too!" Roman says.

I hug them tightly against me.

Daphne wraps her arms around the three of us and envelopes me and our children with love.

I miss you, Dad. I miss you every day.

I promise I'll do my best to give my children and my wife everything you gave me and Mom.

I'll give them all the love I have.

Want to find out about my next book before everyone else and get free novellas not available anywhere else? Then sign up for my mailing list!

Sign up here and get a FREE novella now!!

http://eepurl.com/B7crf

Personal thanks from Devon Hartford:

Thank you so much for taking the time to live with Apollo and Daphne and their families for a while. If you enjoyed *Taking Back Beautiful*, please leave a review wherever you purchased this ebook, on Goodreads, or any book blogs you frequent. Be sure to tell your friends about it!

Do you want more Apollo & Daphne?

Would you like to read a FULL LENGTH NOVEL about them?

:-) Contact me and tell me about it!! :-)

Like me on Facebook

Friend me on Facebook

Follow me on Twitter @DevonHartford

Follow me on WordPress at devonhartford.com

COVER MODEL

A Steamy Standalone Romantic Comedy
BY DEVON HARTFORD

They called him Connor HUGE.

Connor Hughes f**ked his way through every girl in my high school.

Except me.

We *hated* each other.

That arrogant a**hole insulted me, tormented me, and *ruined* me without ever laying a finger on me.

After graduating near the top of my class, I escaped to UCLA, got my degree, and threw myself into a career as a serious journalist. But I never forgot the damage Connor did.

At least I'll never have to see him again.

Until my editor at *Trending Magazine* tasks me with writing a tell-all article about Connor. Turns out my insufferable bad boy nemesis grew into the ultra-gorgeous model whose perfect body steams up the covers of half the romance novels on the bestseller lists.

Now I'm stuck shadowing him all weekend long at the world's largest Romance Convention. I'm forced to watch in disgust as 45,000 women throw themselves at him and worship his shirtless body while he taunts me incessantly.

We hate each other as much today as we did seven years ago. But I can't stop stealing glances at his perfect abs and perfect a**.

My better judgment tells me to drop everything and run, but

something deep inside me is dying to know if he's as HUGE as the rumors...

Cover Model is a steamy standalone with an HEA

PROLOGUE

ELECTRA

GRAD NIGHT, 2008.

"Not on your life," I chuckle, staring into the most beautiful blue eyes I've ever hated.

I stand toe to toe with Connor Hughes, the gorgeous young man I hate more than any other human being on the planet.

"You totally want me." He flashes his insolent grin, the one that makes all the girls in school drool over him and write his name in their notebooks and stalk his Facebook page in hopes that he'll mention them. "You've *always* wanted me."

My anger rises and I snort, "I've *never* wanted you. *Connor.*" I spit out his name like it's filthy. "You must think I'm pretty stupid if you think I'm going to let myself become yet another notch on your bedpost."

In the distance, a flickering rainbow of lights beam from the grad night carnival set up behind our high school. All that frolic and fun seems a million miles away.

Ten hours ago, Connor and I walked separately across the stage in the North Valley High School gymnasium and got our diplomas from the principal. When Connor got his, he took a bow to an uproar of cheers and applause. Everybody loves Connor Hughes. Except me. When I took my diploma, nobody made a sound, not even the crickets.

Now it's four in the morning and I'm all alone with Connor under the starry night sky.

I fold my arms defensively across my chest and growl in his arrogant and undeniably handsome face. "The only reason you want me is because you never *had* me, *Connor*. We both know that if I was dumb enough to have sex with you, you'd get what you've wanted all along, and you'd move on. Just like you did with every other unsuspecting girl you've fucked. Tell me I'm wrong."

He opens his mouth to speak. A strained half syllable wheezes out but catches in his throat. "I—" He deflates, his muscled shoulders sagging.

"That's what I thought," I smirk. "I'm just another notch for you. But I've got news for you, Connor *Screws*. You will *never* catch me. I will *always* get away. After everything that you've done, I will *never* be one of your notches."

I turn on the heel of my brand new bowtie flats and stride across the damp grass field toward the main parking lot. I never look back, promising myself that I will *never* think about Connor Hughes *ever* again.

As far as I'm concerned, he is out of my life forever.

Good riddance.

CHAPTER 1

CONNOR

SEVEN YEARS LATER…

"Fuck, you're tight," I grunt as I push my dick deeper into her pussy. "And wet as fuck."

We're sprawled on the king-sized hotel bed where we've been fuckin since the sun came up.

Her eyes are clamped shut and her face is screwed up as tight as her pussy. "Ohhhh, yes, Connor, yes…" she moans. "I'm going to come again…"

They always do.

This will be her fourth orgasm this morning, and the seventh since last night when we stumbled up to my room.

I slam into her harder and harder. "Squeeze my dick, babe. Fuckin *squeeze* it… Yeah…"

Her mouth splits open and she cries out, "*Yes, yes, oh my god, yes!!*" Her nails claw my shoulders. This chick's a fuckin beast between the sheets.

I'm down with that. "Come on my dick, Juh—" I stop myself because I almost said Jasmine. She doesn't notice. I don't think this chick's name is Jasmine. Jasmine was Tuesday. At least I *think* it was Jasmine. Or was Jasmine on Wednesday and Siobhan was Tuesday?

Who knows.

I should just stick to calling all of them Babe.

The only thing I do remember about this chick is that she told me earlier she's half Chinese and half Brazilian. Exotic as hell. Long black hair, tanned caramel skin, perfect bod, killer tits. Crazy hot. You don't come across a chick like this every day, but I'm going to come inside her in a minute.

When she picked me up last night, she was easily the hottest chick in the club. I spotted her out of a sea of plastic Beverly Hills blondes immediately. I grew out of my blonde bimbo phase three years ago. They're usually shitty lays. But this chick around my dick is top shelf. Prime Grade. Just like that choice beef they serve down in the restaurants of Brazil. Or is that Argentina? I can't remember. For me, the month long jungle photo shoot I did down in South America was one big blur of exotic pussy, killer booze, and killer food. The steaks down there are unreal.

I nearly laugh out loud at the thought.

I can't believe I'm thinking about Argentinian beef while I'm fuckin this hottie, but I am. No matter how much I think I'm into a chick, my mind always ends up wandering during sex.

"I'm coming, Connor," she squeals as her pussy grabs my dick like a fist.

Yeah she is.

Time for me to let loose myself and get this over with. I've got shit to do today. I groan wordlessly as I pump harder and shoot a load into the condom. It's good but not great.

It's never great.

But it helps me forget about *her*.

For a minute, anyway.

The second I roll off Babe, or whatever her name is, and close my eyes, I see *her* face.

I fuckin *hate* that.

After seven years, I can't stop thinking about the last time I saw *her* face.

One of these years, I'm going to forget about Electra Warmoth.

Or not.

ELECTRA

I didn't spend four years at UCLA getting a degree in journalism for *this*. Writing an exposé on a male model who poses shirtless for romance novel book covers?

Please.

What about this assignment says serious journalism?

None of it.

Sleek modernist decor on the seventh floor surrounds me as I walk along the luxe patterned carpeting toward my destination. Early morning light shines through windows at the end of the long hallway, stabbing my eyes. I need coffee. It's way too early for this nonsense.

I'm beyond irritated about being here.

Why?

Late last night, Vince Pitts, my annoying ass of a Managing Editor over at *Trending Magazine,* insisted I cover this silly story if I wanted to keep getting work from him. I'm a freelancer, and only a junior contributor at that, which means I barely scrape by on what I earn. Considering I still owe a king's ransom on my student loans from getting my journalism degree at UCLA, I agreed. So here I am at Rom Com Con 2015, short for Romantic Comedy Convention, which takes place every summer at the sprawling Beverly Hills Resort and Convention Center.

Can you say waste of time?

I told Vince I didn't care that there will be over a hundred hot hard-bodied male cover models circulating throughout the convention for the next three days, signing autographs and showing off their flawless physiques. I reminded him that a few weeks ago, Hilary Clinton announced her candidacy for President. Whether I agree with her politics or not, I should be following *her* on the campaign trail, covering *her* story as she sets *her* sights on making feminist history. It's about time this country had a woman for president.

But *nooooo*, Vince insisted I spend my Fourth of July weekend here covering this trivial fluff piece. The only fireworks I'm going to see are the irritated ones shooting out of my ears.

Walking beside me in the hotel hallway is a guy named Romeo Fabiano. He's slightly shorter than I am, has olive skin, a coifed black faux-hawk, and a perpetual grin. As we walk, a slick black vinyl trench coat billows out behind him and a monocle bounces from a black string tied to one of his vest's many buckles. Emo chic. He and I met for the first time this morning. Margaret Lang, my media contact for the convention, introduced me to Romeo when I arrived at the resort. She instructed him to take me up to the interview.

"Are you excited to meet him?" Romeo titters. "I know *I* am."

"Excited?" I sigh. "Why should I be excited?"

"Because *no one* has ever seen *HIS* face."

"Maybe *HIS* face isn't worth seeing," I mock, picturing some random meathead gym rat with a dopey expression and a crooked nose whose only asset is his body.

"Surely you jest," Romeo says. "We're talking about *the* Connor. The hottest male model in the business. The man with the perfect body. The body by which all others are measured and found lacking."

The sour expression on my face says: *I don't care.* I could be reporting on the plight of displaced refugees in third world countries. Instead, I'm here at Rom Com Con covering *this*. Open disdain shows on my face. Poker is not my game. But I am a professional, so I try to think happy thoughts to smooth out my wrinkled brow. It doesn't work.

Romeo drives his point home. "A *Connor Cover*, as they're known in the industry, practically guarantees that a book will sell millions of copies and land a top ten slot on The New York Times best sellers list. His abs put washboards out of business. His chest makes granite statues weep with envy. His shoulders made Atlas shrug in defeat. And those tattooed arms? Mmm-mmm, girl. With a body like his, I can only imagine what his *heads* look like."

"You mean, 'head'," I correct.

"No, I mean *heads*. As in, plural. As in, both of them…" His eyes flicker impishly.

I refrain from rolling mine, but the urge is intense. "I hate to break it to you, but the logical conclusion why he's never shown his face is because it's not worth showing."

Romeo nods, "There's been endless speculation on the fan blogs about whether he's handsome or heinous."

"I vote heinous. He's probably a troll. With two troll heads growing from his shoulders."

"O, ye of little faith," Romeo snickers while pulling out a smart phone. He taps the screen and shows me an image. It's a shirtless and headless male torso on the cover of some random book called *Stepbrother Obsessed*. I have no idea what that is. Sounds pornographic. But there's no denying the perfection of the body I'm looking at. It's hard, cut, masculine, inked, and it makes something squirm between my legs, something I thought was either hibernating or flat out extinct.

"You're blush-*iiiing*," Romeo singsongs.

"No I'm not," I bark. I clear my throat and try to sound professional. Yes, I can appreciate a gorgeous body as much as the next woman or obviously gay man like Romeo. But I've always preferred brains over beefcake. "Who is this Connor guy again? Does he have a last name?"

"Nobody knows what it is. He's very protective of his anonymity. Some people believe Connor isn't his real first name at all."

That's no help. I sigh heavily, "Look, my editor literally gave me this assignment last night and I didn't have time to research Connor *Whoever*." The truth is, I didn't *want* to do any research because this is such a meaningless non-story. It's not like interviewing a headless male model with no last name at Rom Com Con 2015 is going to win me a Pulitzer. "So unfortunately I don't know the first thing about this guy. Can you fill me in?"

"Don't you *read*?" Romeo gasps. "Connor is *the* thing in the romance books business."

"I read the Wall Street Journal and Ms. Magazine. Not frivolous romance novels filled with gratuitous sex. I know about 50 Shades of Grey."

"Your loss," Romeo shrugs. "Sounds to me like you could use some frivolity and gratuity in your life."

"What's that supposed to mean?!" I bark.

"Here we *ARE-rreeee*!" Romeo sings, ignoring me.

We stand in front of room 714.

"Are you ready to meet him?" Romeo asks anxiously, his eyes shining gleefully. "I know I am."

"I guess." I fold my arms across my chest and shift my weight impatiently onto the heel of one pump.

"The man of my dreams is on the other side of that door." Romeo beams while he knocks. "Do you think he'll be wearing a mask? Like a sexy but mysterious professional wrestler?"

I didn't realize professional wrestlers were sexy. As before, I try to keep my confrontational comments to myself. I reach into my conservative purse and flick the power button on my mp3 voice recorder to make sure the battery is still good. It is. Distracted, I ask, "Why would he be wearing a mask?"

"Maybe he's horribly disfigured like *The Phantom of the Opera*. Yes, that's it! Once a dashing young man, he lost his looks in a tragic opera fire."

"Opera fire?" I ask doubtfully.

"Yes, bear with me," Romeo says seriously. "Now he's wounded, his heart damaged beyond repair. He yearns in secret for the love of a strong young woman to save him from his solitary misery!" Romeo's eyes light victoriously.

"You're hopeless, Romeo," I chuckle.

"I know, right?" he smiles and winks at me. "Now *THE* Connor is finally going to make his first *ever* public appearance this afternoon, mask and all, exclusively for Rom Com Con 2015!!!"

I arch an eyebrow.

"It's an historic event," he says seriously.

"*An* historic event?" I mock. *A woman president would be an historic event.*

"That's what I said. Did I misspeak?"

Misspeak? Romeo is definitely in a class by himself. I frown at him and nod toward the door. "Never mind. Let's get this over with. Let's meet *THE* Connor."

Romeo knocks on the door and we wait.

And wait.

Wait a second…

No way.

A jumble of loose thoughts suddenly straighten in my mind. It's just a coincidence, right? Thousands of men are named Connor. It seems highly unlikely that *this* Connor is…*him.*

Connor Hughes.

I haven't seen or heard from Connor in seven years. I haven't even thought about him…

Dark memories lasso my guts and cinch tight. I wince internally, forcing down nausea, not letting it show. I never let it show.

Keeping a straight face doesn't stop the distressed thoughts from pinballing around in my head.

It can't be him…

CONNOR

"I can't believe how good you are in bed, Connor," Babe, or whatever her name is, says breathlessly. "I've never had so many orgasms in one morning." Her lush lips spread into a grin.

Mine don't.

I stand naked at the foot of the bed having just dumped my condom in the bathroom trash.

Babe is a vision of caramel delight on the rumpled white confection of the hotel sheets.

I couldn't care less.

She runs her hands across her breasts, massaging them briefly before sliding her manicured fingers down her taut stomach and between her slick thighs, stroking herself invitingly. She locks eyes with me, hers half-hooded with naked desire for more. "Mmmmm, Connor. Do you have any idea how yummy you are?"

Yes. Some other chick called me yummy last week. Yummy turned into a chick cliché four years ago. I hear it all the time.

"Your cock is twitching. Does that mean you want to go again?" she purrs.

I'm always up for fuckin. Working out seven days a week makes me horny as fuck all the time. And I have to admit, Babe is fuckin hot. But hasn't she had enough of me? I've had enough of her. As hot as she is, she just didn't do it for me. They never do. I sigh, "I don't mean to be a dick, but I have an interview here in the room in a few minutes. I need to clean up before they get here."

"Interview? For what?"

"It's nothing. Some, uhhh, fitness thing," I lie. "Some guy's YouTube workout channel."

"That sounds exciting."

I always tell girls I'm a fitness model, but I never go into more detail than that. I hate talking about myself. "It's pretty boring. Kind of technical. Blood sugar levels, triglycerides, recovery intervals. Boring shit like that." Usually the technical talk turns them off.

"I don't mind," Babe purrs. "I'm sure I'll learn something."

Maybe this chick has potential…

She does that stripper thing where she sticks out the tip of her tongue and runs it across her top teeth. When that doesn't work, she tweaks one of her nipples with her fingers, lifts her tit to her mouth, and licks the nip.

…Then again, maybe not.

Why'd she have to go and ruin it?

"Trust me," I chuckle, "You'll be snoring inside of two minutes. And the guy is a nobody. I think his biggest video has like 700 views. I'm doing it as a favor for a friend." I'm making all of this up as I go along. Babe will never know.

"It's no big deal, Connor. I really don't mind."

This always happens. A girl like her has guys throwing themselves at her 24/7. I saw it at the club last night. Five hundred different guys talked to her, but she went back to the hotel with me. What should've been a one-nighter is suddenly turning into a pain in my ass. I don't know how to break it to her that I'm not interested. After fuckin them, I never am.

So, how to get rid of her?

Usually, I like the direct approach.

"You need to go," I grunt.

ELECTRA

Romeo leans his ear against the door, "I don't hear anyone inside. Do you have a drinking glass?"

"Why?"

"So I can hear better. Don't you watch spy movies?" he hisses.

"Not really."

"Which celebrity do you think he looks like?" Romeo muses gleefully, his ear still glued to the door.

"I have no idea." Nor do I care. My kind of man has a career path. Soft porn modeling is *not* a career path. Nothing gets me going like a suit and tie. Not that I've had anything going on in the boyfriend or the bedroom department since forever. I'm focused on being a journalist, not meaningless flings.

"Whatever he looks like," Romeo swoons, "I bet he's gorgeous. I'm picturing chiseled cheek bones, a brooding brow, smoldering eyes, and a rugged stubbled jaw."

I smirk, "That sounds like a caveman or a neanderthal. Does he wear a leopard skin for a loincloth and carry a club too?"

"I hope so," Romeo grins, his eyes dreamy. "Then he can pound me with his club, take me back to his cave, and pound me with his *human* club from behi—"

"Stop!" I bark.

"Never mind me," he giggles. "A serious woman like you is only interested in serious information, right?"

"What makes you think I'm serious?" I ask defensively.

His eyes sweep up and down my outfit. One of his eyebrows arches dramatically and his face says, *Have you looked in a mirror lately?* But his mouth says, "Please, girlfriend. Your outfit was on the cover of the latest issue of Business Matron's Monthly."

I hide my scowl as I look down my nose at him through my stylish eyeglasses. "That's not even a real magazine." My long auburn hair may be pinned up in a conservative bun, but I look good in my pumps, pencil skirt, and blouse. I always dress my best so people take me seriously.

"We'll work on tomorrow's look later," he smiles. "But we can do something about that uptight hair of yours." He reaches for my bun like he's going to fiddle with it, or worse, let it down completely. "Your hair bun is so tight it's giving you a facelift."

"Hands off!" I growl, pulling back defensively. He thinks he can give *me* fashion advice? He looks like a cartoon character. I resist the urge to kick his shins with my pointed pumps.

He drops his arm to his side, "Loosen up, girl. I'm just trying to help."

"What do you know about women's fashion? Look at *your* outfit! I didn't realize sci-fi emo was still a *thing*," I spit. "And what's with that stupid monocle?"

With practiced flair, he flips the monocle up with a flick of his wrist and squinches it in his cheek. He stares at me through it, the monocled eye comically magnified. "Perhaps you need a personality makeover, darling," he mutters before letting the monocle tumble free.

I'm about to give him a tongue lashing when I stop myself. I admit it. I'm very sensitive about my looks, my personality, everything. Let's face it. I'm just plain sensitive. I blame four years of high school torment from Connor Hughes. That asshole left me scarred.

That's when the hotel room door suddenly whips open and my chest locks down tight, stopping my breath.

It's him.

Connor Hughes.

No. Fucking. Way.

COVER MODEL
by Devon Hartford
AVAILABLE NOW!!

ABOUT THE AUTHOR

Devon Hartford spent most of his life in Southern California frequenting many of the locations in Cover Model. Devon is an artist and musician, and drew upon his experiences with both while writing his previous romance series The Story of Samantha Smith and The Story of Victory Payne.

OTHER BOOKS BY DEVON HARTFORD:

ROMANTIC COLLEGE COMEDY
Fearless (The Story of Samantha Smith #1)
Reckless (The Story of Samantha Smith #2)
Painless (The Story of Samantha Smith #3)

ROMANTIC NEW ADULT COMEDY
COVER MODEL
Taking Back Beautiful

ROMANTIC HIGH SCHOOL COMEDY
Stepbrother Obsessed

NEW ADULT ROMANCE
Stealing Chastity

BILLIONAIRE ROMANCE
ONE YEAR LOVE - Part One
ONE YEAR LOVE - Part Two
ONE YEAR LOVE - Part Three
ONE YEAR LOVE - Part Four
ONE YEAR LOVE - Collected Edition (Parts 1-4)

ROCKER ROMANCE
Victory RUN 1 (The Story of Victory Payne)
Victory RUN 2 (The Story of Victory Payne)
Victory RUN 3 (The Story of Victory Payne)
Victory RUN 1-2-3 (The Story of Victory Payne - Collecting Parts 1-2-3)

ACKNOWLEDGMENTS

A HUGE thanks to:

Jackie Barnett for her usual genius

Bethanie "The Typo Hammer" Melander for killing those typos

Her Highness Samantha Sheeley (Queen of All Typos) for all the Oopsies!

An even HUGER thanks to all my passionate and fantastic beta readers:

Steffini Walker Texas Ranger, Rosanne Triegaardt, Stephanie Svajgl, Wendy Boyer, Mandy Jamerson, The REAL Julie England, Natasha Slater, Tania Clark, Megan C Christmas, Tamara Clark, Sandy England, Juliana the Blue Bomber, Maria Combee, Michele McKenzie, Nicki Hewitt-Hart, Sarah Frost

Jessie Duchannes for her awesome reviews and Sailor Moon.

Hayley Picknell for slick Brit Pimpin' and awesome reviews everywhere!

Michele McKenzie for equally all-star pimpin' and typo-snyping.

Amy Cossio for always rocking the Awesome Saucio.

And last but not least, for last minute typo-snyping of the highest order and in the face of great personal danger, I award a Typo Heart to **Colonel Melanie Starr,** the one and only **Comma Bomber,** who saved this mission from certain disaster at the 11th hour, but not without significant personal sacrifice on her part. Colonel, I salute you!

Thanks to everybody else who has helped make this book a reality!